# FIGHT BACK

**BRENT R. SHERRARD**

James Lorimer & Company Ltd., Publishers
Toronto

James Lorimer & Company Ltd., Publishers acknowledges the support of the Ontario Arts Council. We acknowledge the financial support of the Government of Canada through the Canada Book Fund for our publishing activities. We acknowledge the support of the Canada Council for the Arts which last year invested $24.3 million in writing and publishing throughout Canada. We acknowledge the Government of Ontario through the Ontario Media Development Corporation's Ontario Book Initiative.

ONTARIO ARTS COUNCIL
CONSEIL DES ARTS DE L'ONTARIO

The Canada Council | Le Conseil des Arts
for the Arts | du Canada

Canadä

Cover design: Meredith Bangay
Cover image: Shutterstock

Library and Archives Canada Cataloguing in Publication

Sherrard, Brent R., author
    Fight back / Brent R. Sherrard.

Issued in print and electronic formats
ISBN978-1-4594-0859-3(bound).--ISBN978-1-4594-0858-6(pbk.).--
ISBN 978-1-4594-0860-9 (epub)

    I. Title.

PS8637.H488F53 2015          jC813'.6          C2014-907545-6
C2014-907546-4

James Lorimer & Company Ltd.,          Distributed in the United States by:
Publishers                             Orca Book Publishers
317 Adelaide Street West, Suite 1002   P.O. Box 468
Toronto, ON, Canada                    Custer, WA USA
M5V 1P9                                98240-0468
www.lorimer.ca

Printed and bound in Canada
Manufactured by Marquis in Montmagny, Quebec in February 2015.
Job # 111639

# FIGHT BACK

**ALSO BY BRENT R. SHERRARD
IN THE SIDESTREETS SERIES:**

*Final Takedown*
*Wasted*

*For everyone who has ever found the*
*courage to fight back*

# PROLOGUE

*It's my seventh birthday, and there's something wrong. There's a cake and balloons and a shiny chrome-and-blue bike. There are other kids running around our yard, laughing and yelling and having fun, just like at a normal birthday party. None of it fits. It's just not right. Dad even seems happy with me, and that's what makes me scared.*

*Mom cuts up the cake and pours us all a plastic cupful of lemonade. I manage to get mine down, although my stomach is flopping. Dad is giving me that look. The one that says I'm about to mess up, and I'll pay for it.*

*"All right everyone, let's watch Tyler ride his new bike," Dad says.*

*He puts the kickstand up and walks the bike over to me. I'm trying to breathe normally as I grab the handlebars and swing my leg over the seat. Everyone is smiling at me as if they know I'm about to mess up. Dad walks over to his pickup truck and stands next to it, nodding and waving me forward. He has left just enough room between himself and the truck for me to cycle by. I wish I could tell him "Please, no," but suddenly he looks angry, and I comply.*

*I stand up on the pedals and start forward. Everything goes well for a few seconds, but then the bike wobbles, and I push hard on the pedals as I try to gain my balance. It doesn't work. It just makes things worse. Now I've got a choice: hit either Dad or the truck. I crash into the truck and the kids all laugh. I've never ridden a bike before.*

*I pick myself up, ignoring the pain in my knee, and stand the bike up. Dad grabs it and tosses it into the bed of the truck. The laughter stops as he glares at me, and I stare at the ground and wait for what's coming.*

*"Did you ever see such an idiot?" he asks. Nobody answers. He places his hand on his belt buckle and my stomach feels sick.*

*"Tyler's a idiot," my little sister, Rachel, chirps.*

*"All right, party's over," Dad says. "I'll talk to you later, idiot."*

*I go to my room and wait. That's the hardest part, waiting. The afternoon passes, and the evening shadows cross my wall. I pray that he gets caught drinking and driving again, or even that he's killed in an accident. As darkness approaches I know he won't be far behind. I hear the truck, and then the kitchen door slams with a brutal promise.*

*My door opens, and I can tell he's drunk by the way he stands, before I even smell the booze. He slides his belt free, doubling it up and slapping it on his thigh. I'm just glad this didn't happen in front of the other kids.*

*"Drop 'em," he slurs. "I don't know what's wrong with you, boy."*

*I don't know either.*

# 1

## INFIGHTING

I grew up hating bullies. Anyone who picks on someone, just because they can, is a coward. I hated the way they could sense your fear, and how it made them stronger. There are two ways to handle being picked on. One is to lie down and give up. The other is to get angry and fight back. As I got older I used the hurt and anger to fight back. Not against my dad, because he would've killed me. But anyone else who ever messed with me only did it once.

One day while I was at school Mom and my little sister, Rachel, went for a drive. They never came back. Mom called that evening, telling Dad that she'd had enough and was moving back to her family in Maine. I didn't really care. Her two loves in life were Rachel and vodka anyway. The bad part was being left alone with an angry drunk guy.

Later that night, in a booze-fuelled rage, Dad demanded to know why I hadn't told him about Mom's plan to take off. I told him the truth — that she hadn't said a word to me about her plan. He called me a liar, and then he punched me in the mouth.

One of my front teeth snapped off, and another one was driven sideways through my lip, splitting it wide open. It bled like a tap, and it took me ten minutes to clean up the trail I'd left from the kitchen to the bathroom. But I didn't cry. I was eleven years old.

The next morning I got ready and left for school, as usual, except this time I had a plan. The teacher took one look at my face and escorted me to the principal's office. I told him my Dad had done it. I was taking a huge risk telling the truth, but it paid off. The principal called Child Protection, and when I'd told them what happened they placed me in a group home. After two weeks, and numerous fist fights, they sent me to live with Dad's mother. I felt like an orphan. I also felt safe for the first time in my life. Gram and Dad hated each other and hadn't spoken in years. I figured he was glad to be rid of me, and Gram's was the last place he would think to look anyway. Even if he cared where I was, he wouldn't think to look for me there.

She tried to talk to me, but it was a waste of time. I didn't think she was qualified to tell me how to live, seeing as she hadn't done such a great job raising my father. With me at school, and her spending most evenings at bingo, at least I didn't have to put up with her very much.

I'd moved to Gram's house on a Thursday and wouldn't have to face the prospect of starting at a new school until Monday. That gave me three days to explore my new territory and see what the odds were of picking up some work after school and on weekends. Every neighbourhood had elderly folks who needed odd jobs done. If you were polite, and they considered you trustworthy, the pay was really good.

There was a shed behind Gram's house, and I decided to check it out. Walking up to the door, I took a deep breath and yanked it open. I jumped back, a shiver racing up my spine. I glanced behind me, but I wasn't back home, and Dad wasn't about to pounce. Peering into the gloom, all I saw were soggy cardboard boxes and a rusty lawn mower.

My new bedroom was upstairs in Gram's tumbledown farmhouse, just outside of town. It smelled mouldy, so I searched for some air freshener. In the bathroom, under the sink, I found a full quart of rum and a handgun. It was a six-shooter, cowboy style, and I could see bullets in the cylinder. I aimed it at the wall between my bedroom and myself, and I pulled the trigger. There was a deafening explosion as a perfect hole appeared in the wallpaper. I pictured Dad's forehead.

I returned to my room, finding a handful of plaster and splintered wood all over my bed. Since Gram couldn't get up the stairs on account of her bad knees, I didn't need to worry about getting into trouble. I put the gun and booze away in my closet.

I spent Saturday repairing and painting Mrs. Malley's backyard fence, scoring forty bucks for six hours of work. The next weekend I'd be trimming bushes and cleaning windows and such for her friend, Mrs. Delroy, another widow. I knew there'd be lots of jobs shovelling walkways in the coming winter, too.

Sunday morning Gram went to church, and I slept until ten. After lunch she went off to the afternoon bingo, and I decided to explore the back of her property. It was mostly pasture overgrown with raspberry bushes and alders, and an abandoned shale rock pit which bordered the Cleeland River.

I found a place to sit, watching the river flow past. After a few minutes I started feeling relaxed, and then a beer bottle floated by.

It reminded me of Dad, and how booze always came first, and before I knew it I was in a rage. I wished I could get into a fight. It was the only way I knew to express my anger and hate. And I didn't even care if I won.

Back at the house I cooked myself pancakes for supper and watched a little television. I drifted off, and when I heard the door shut I sprang out of my chair. It would take a while to get used to being safe.

"What's wrong with you? Are you on dope or what?" Gram said.

"No, I fell asleep. I didn't know . . ." I began.

"Never mind," she said. "You just make sure you keep it together at school, you hear me? Keep your mouth shut and your head down. I won't be putting up with any foolishness, and maybe you could get that hair cut. What are you, a girl?"

Dad had made me grow my hair long because he'd said that if I was going to act like a girl, I might as well look like one. He used to threaten to put ribbons in it and send me to school. He never did — he knew that just the threat alone kept me nervous.

"I'm going to my room, I'll see you in the morning," I said.

"The bus goes by at eight, be waiting when it gets here. And don't wake me up, you hear? Heed my words, Tyler, and try to fit in, or it'll be back to the home for you."

"Yeah," I said.

\*\*\*

I woke up with butterflies in my stomach, dreading my first day as the new kid at school. As a mid-term arrival I'd stick out like a third eyeball. For sure there'd be someone wanting to put me in my place.

By the time I'd made my way downstairs I'd accepted the day's promise of violence. I knew if nobody started anything, I would anyway. Waiting for something bad to happen was second nature to me. I had a bowl of cereal, then sat on the step and watched for the bus.

As soon as I climbed aboard I saw him. He was close to the back, sprawled across a seat, with a tough-guy sneer and his foot thrown across the aisle.

There were lots of seats up front, but that would have been like backing down. He looked to be a few years older than me and was definitely bigger. He looked puzzled as I walked back the aisle toward him.

"Move your foot, dickhead," I said calmly.

"You little shit, I'll . . ." he began. The words meant nothing. Not moving his foot meant everything. The thing about punks is, they like to bluff. I'm not a punk. I smashed a left into his face, driving his head back. He tried to get up, but I was raining punches on him, and he leaned sideways and covered up.

I stopped punching, but he stayed safe and didn't move. I walked back up the aisle and sat down, the bus so quiet I could hear people breathing. I figured it was a pretty good start.

# 2

# BRAWLER

When I got to school I went straight to the office to announce my arrival. The receptionist gave me the number of my homeroom class and said she was sure that I'd enjoy my time at Northridge Junior High School. She hoped that I would feel at home here, she said. I told her that the last thing I needed was to feel *at home* while I wasn't at home.

I had twenty minutes until class started, so I went outside and found a spot where I could get my back against a wall and look things over.

There was a large group of Goths over by

the soccer nets, clumped together like a flock of ravens. The well-off kids, with their perfect teeth and fancy clothes, gathered near the entrance doors, feeling safe being so close to authority.

Then there were the tough kids, hanging around the perimeter fence, as far from school as they could get. They were like wolves, watching for weaklings to take down. The ones who were already pretty well defeated by their lives and seemed to be begging for someone to pick on them. I watched as a guy who looked like he was way too old for junior high kicked a skinny little kid's books out from under his arm. He and his friends hooted and laughed while their victim meekly gathered everything back up. I felt the blood leaving my face and my hands getting really hot.

I followed the kid who'd had his books kicked out from under his arm until we were out of sight of the tough guys. Hustling up behind him, I tapped him on the shoulder. He spun around to face me, his eyes wide with fear.

"Give them to me," I demanded.

"What?" he squeaked.

"The books. Give me your books," I said. I didn't have time to explain what I had planned as he passed them over, his hands trembling. I wondered how it was possible that someone could have absolutely no fight in them.

My old man used to take me out with him, partying and drinking and, plenty of times, brawling. He'd tell Mom that we were going to the stock-car races or a hockey game, whatever, and then we'd head for a drinking party somewhere. We wouldn't get home until two or three o'clock in the morning. I would lie right along with him about the truck breaking down, or getting stuck, as an excuse for being so late.

Lots of times at those parties there'd be a drunken argument, and the fists and blood would fly. I'd seen Dad in action lots of times, and he always hit first and often and hard. It was just like he'd gone mad, his eyes all wild and spit spraying from between his clenched teeth.

"Make sure they know you're crazy, so no one else will want to jump in. Hit them first, and make sure they stay hit," he'd say.

I tucked everything under my arm and then casually strolled past the tough guys. I wasn't halfway by them when a foot flew out from the crowd and drove the books out of my grip.

I turned around and calmly told the guy who did it to pick them up. The laughter died quickly as he exchanged looks of disbelief with his buddies.

"How would you like me to kick *you* all over this parking lot, you skinny piece of shit," he said with a smirk. I smashed a left hand into his eye, knocking the smirk from his face. I grabbed his ear with my right hand and hit him twice more before we tumbled to the pavement. As soon as we landed someone kicked me in the back, knocking the wind out of me.

He was much bigger than I was, and the only fighting I was doing was for my next breath. He quickly got on top of me and started smashing punches into my face. I heard the dull thuds of his fists hitting me, but I felt no pain. Suddenly his body flew backwards, and I jumped up to face an extremely red-faced man in glasses, shirt, and tie.

"Are you crazy?" he said. "I watched the whole thing from the lobby. You did that on purpose. You borrowed those books just so he would kick them out of your arms, didn't you?"

The guy I'd been fighting with had moved right next to the pencil-neck who was glaring at me over his glasses, and started whining about just having fun, and me hitting him first. I stepped forward and smashed him in the eye again, which was already swelling up pretty good. Judging by the tight feeling around my cheekbones, so was my face.

He fell to the ground, clutching his eye and yelling, while the guy in the necktie pushed me backwards and yelled, "Stop! Stop it! What's wrong with you?"

"There's nothing wrong with me," I said.

I followed him into the school, where I was

ordered to sit in a chair and told to wait. After ten minutes the receptionist directed me to the vice-principal's office. The vice-principal was the guy from outside.

"Welcome to Northridge Junior High, Tyler. I can see that your time with us promises to be interesting, to say the least," he said. "Would you care to explain your actions?"

"No," I replied.

I ended up getting suspended for two weeks, which I figured could be worth a couple of hundred bucks in odd jobs. It was fall, and there were countless things people needed done before winter set in. Plus I could read what I wanted, when I wanted, instead of sitting in class trying to listen to bullshit that meant nothing to me.

Of course Gram freaked, told me that I was going to turn out to be no good, like her son, and that if I messed up again I could hit the road. I wondered what security would feel like, if I could even handle it. Mom had always threatened to walk out, from as far back as I could recall. I had never known if she meant to take Rachel and me with her or not. Dad did take off from time to time but always came back when he ran out of money, or so Mom said.

By the time I got back to school I'd earned two hundred and forty bucks, and the bruises on my face had finally disappeared. I'd looked really weird right at the end, with banana-coloured stains from my chin to my eyebrows. I was just sorry that I didn't get to see what the other guy looked like.

# 3

## ON QUEER STREET

So I kept to myself, managed to get passing grades, and basically just drifted along. Gram and I lived in the same house, but we rarely saw each other or spoke when we did. I liked it that way.

I moved on to Langston High School in grade nine, and by the time I entered grade ten I'd started hanging out with a few guys from school. Not a lot, but we'd kick around in our spare time once in a while, enough for me to discover weed. Billy Turnbull would wait until his dad passed out and score a few grams from his stash. We'd all smoke up, and they'd laugh themselves into spasms at the slightest prompting. I'd get to thinking about forever and infinity. I'd wonder, where did everything end, or begin?

As soon as I found my own source for weed, I started to withdraw into my own world again. I began to spend all of my spare time getting high, alone in my room, reading and thinking. The more I tried to understand Dad's cruelty to me, the angrier I grew. I started getting more and more upset, and spent countless evenings pacing around the old house until I was dizzy.

With no one to talk to, and no one to turn to but myself, I should've known I was aiming for trouble. Then one Saturday night, ripped on Afghan Skunk, I remembered the rum and the gun, and then not much else until I came to in the hospital.

"Glad to see you're awake," said the police officer seated by my bed. "You're under arrest."

"For what?" I managed to croak before I

had to stop and fight back the urge to puke. I was sticky with sweat, and my mouth felt like a dry sponge.

"Let's see, now," he replied. "There's illegal possession of alcohol, marijuana, and a restricted weapon. And pointing that same weapon at a police officer. And uttering death threats to that same officer. You're lucky to be alive, son, Granville was seconds away from putting you down. And then, when you passed out and hit the pavement, that damned pistol you were holding fired. Is that enough for now?"

Just then a nurse entered the room with a cup of water and two pills. The officer asked her to witness him reading me my rights, then he left, mumbling about not knowing what to do.

"The doctor says you'll be released tomorrow morning," he said, sticking his head back in the door. "We'll see what happens then, I guess."

"You just relax, honey. Everything's going

to be fine," the nurse said. "The pills will help you sleep. Try to rest, and think of good things, okay?"

I didn't have anything good to think about, so I tried to remember the night before. I recalled smoking a joint and thinking that it would be a good time to open that rum I'd been hoarding for so long. I also remembered thinking about that party when I was seven, and my bike. That was about it.

I dozed on and off for most of the day, read some magazines the nurses had brought me, and tried to ignore the fact that I'd probably be going to jail. By that night I was feeling much better, at least physically, but I was trembling at the thought of what tomorrow would bring. It reminded me of how I'd felt every day growing up.

I drifted off to sleep thinking that maybe it was time to get over that stuff, to get some sort of plan together for my life. Too bad it was too late.

\*\*\*

It was a long night. I'd fall asleep, then jolt awake, thinking that I was behind a locked closet door. So I spent hours trying to come up with some solution, anything that would make it all just disappear.

Morning finally arrived, and I was able to choke down some egg-like substance and milk for breakfast. As far as I knew, the police would come and get me soon. Then it would be off to jail to await a court appearance. I was wrong.

The doctor pronounced me well enough to be released, and I asked for my clothes. The nurse informed me that what I'd been wearing was covered in vomit, but that she'd get me a new outfit from my stuff downstairs. Before I could ask her *what* stuff downstairs, she was gone. Since I couldn't remember much, my only guess was that I'd packed my things and had been running away when the police found me. I wondered where my money was.

The nurse returned with fresh clothes and said that someone would be along shortly to explain everything to me. I'd just gotten dressed when there was a knock at my door. I looked up to see a lady with a briefcase in her hand and a big plastic smile on her face.

"Good morning, Tyler," she said. "My name is Mary Clark, and I'm from the Department of Social Services. I've been assigned as your caseworker. I guess the first order of business is to tell you that your grandmother no longer wishes to have you reside with her. We'll find you a new place to live, so don't you worry, okay?"

I couldn't say I was surprised, and at least it sounded like I wasn't going directly to jail. Still, I'd miss that old house, I'd been safe there.

"So . . . what happens now?" I asked.

"Well, Tyler, right now you and I are going to the police station, and then my office. We'll see about finding you a new home. That's our first priority. Actually, our staff is working on it right now, so just relax. Are you ready to go?"

We collected my belongings from the lobby — my whole life in three garbage bags. After piling them into her trunk, we drove to the cop station, where I was formally charged. Then we went to her office, where she started asking me a lot of questions. I started getting aggravated, and she explained that the questioning was necessary so that they could determine how best to deal with my case.

"The only way you're going to help me is if you can rewind the clock back to Saturday night, and give me a chance to start over again," I said.

"Now, Tyler, we all make mistakes. We just have to deal with them in a rational manner. This could be the beginning of a new and exciting phase in your life."

"Just find me a place to sleep until they lock me up, okay? This isn't a learning experience, you know. I've been an idiot all of my life, and I wish that cop *had* pulled the trigger."

"Don't talk like that, Tyler," she said. "My goodness, there are people who care about you. Think how they'd feel."

"Don't tell me there are people who care about me. You see how quickly my grandmother dropped me? Did you know that when I was eleven my mom took off with my little sister and left me behind with my alcoholic father? My alcoholic and abusive father? I haven't heard from her since. And don't tell me you care, because you get paid to *pretend* you care."

"I'm sorry you feel that way, Tyler. I know that you've had a rough go of it, but a person has to make up their mind to move on. I think that right now could be that time for you. Don't you agree?"

She smiled at me, waiting for a response. I stared at the floor, and she sighed sadly. She claimed she needed a coffee, and asked me if I wanted anything. I said water.

Mary seemed to be gone a long time, but I'd learned years before how to sit still for long periods of time without going insane. That was from one of Dad's favourite punishments — locking me in a dark closet. I occupied the rest of my wait with visions of my fists smashing over and over again into his face.

"Here you go," Mary said, breezing into the room and handing me a bottle of water. I drained half of it in one shot. Suddenly I was so hungry my stomach started to burn.

"I'm starving," I said.

"Me too. Let's go eat," she replied. "Then there's someone I'd like you to talk to. Don't get upset, but I think it's a good idea, and it's required, you know, since you mentioned wishing you'd been shot. It's my duty to report that. It'll only take about half an hour. He's a psychologist, and it's for your own safety. I'd hate to see anything happen to you, Tyler. All right?"

"Great," I replied. It sounded like a good trade. I would talk to this guy, and get a meal for my trouble.

We ate at a fast-food place, stuffing our-selves on fries, cheeseburgers, and onion rings, washed down with watery cola. Driv-ing across town I prepared myself to confront some guy who thought he was smart enough to know what I was thinking.

# 4

## ON THE ROPES

We pulled into the parking lot of an office building. As we walked toward the entryway I hoped I wasn't making a mistake. Anyway, I would just tell him what he wanted to hear.

We took the elevator up to the third floor, and Mary left me in the waiting room while she went to talk to the psychologist. I watched her walk down the quiet hallway, and she was only four doors away when she stopped and knocked on one. Perfect. As soon as she disappeared inside, I hustled down the carpeted hall. Casually leaning against the door frame, I could hear every word clearly.

". . . you think, Mary? I trust your feelings on these things, so give me your honest opinion," I heard a man say.

"I think he's one of the lost ones, Franklin. You know, just drifting along with no direction. There's no police file on him, but I spoke with two of his teachers before I picked him up. He grew up with an alcoholic mother and father, and the father was known to be quite abusive. Tyler would miss school for days and then show up bruised and sore, with a story about an accident of some sort. It should've been looked into, but . . . you know how it goes sometimes."

"Yes, unfortunately," he replied.

"Well, that was about it, until he was eleven. Seems his mother took off for her family home in Maine, taking his little sister along with her. Tyler was left behind with his father, who assaulted him that very same night. That was how he ended up in the system."

"And this is the first time he's been in trouble with the law?"

"Yes, apparently. He's fought all his life and never had any friends — he's always been a loner. He's quite intelligent — I guess he likes to read — and he seems well spoken for his age and background. He won't make eye contact; it's like he's totally self-contained. It's not uncommon for abused children to detach, as I'm sure you're aware."

"Go on," said the doctor.

"Well, after his teacher reported her suspicions of abuse, regarding the injuries to his face, an investigation was initiated. It resulted in his removal from the father's home. There was a short placement in a group home, where he fought often, and then he came here to Trenton. He resided with his paternal grandmother until the incident Saturday night. She dropped his clothes off at the hospital, and that's that. I don't know, Franklin, I just think he deserves a break. I think he's highly redeemable."

"Do you think he's suicidal?"

"Probably not, but you know policy. If anything were to happen, even an attempt, and it was found out that I had been aware of it, well, I'd be held accountable. I'm just covering myself here, Franklin. You know what it's like."

"I know, all too well, Mary, and I agree. You did the right thing in bringing him here. That's all I need for now. I've got an appointment in an hour, but send him in."

When she came out of the office I was sitting where she'd left me.

"Is there a washroom around here?" I said.

"Try to be quick, Tyler, the doctor is very busy," she said.

I hung out in the washroom until there was a knock on the door. "Tyler, are you all right? The doctor is waiting for you!"

"Just a moment," I replied. I'd just been in the process of checking out my teeth, the ones nobody ever saw. The one that had been driven through my lip was tilted back and to the side from that punch years before. I'd noticed that in the last six months or so it had started turning a strange shade of grey, and sometimes the gums around it turned purple and swelled up. At those times, like right now, it was so loose that it seemed like I could have wiggled it loose with my fingers.

I left the bathroom and Mary walked me to the office door, saying that she'd wait for me. I thanked her, knocked on the slightly opened door, and entered the office without waiting for a reply. It was really nice, with paintings on the walls of outdoor scenes, seascapes and such. There were degrees on the walls too, and numerous smiling photographs of the doctor with important-looking people.

"Tyler, how are you?" he said as he rose and came around the desk to shake my hand. Perfect fingernails, and he smelled like a woman. He also had the fakest hair I'd ever seen.

"I'm fine, thank you," I replied.

"Please, have a seat," he said. "So, Mary tells me you had a little trouble on the weekend, that you're feeling a little down. Is that correct?"

"Yeah, but not a little trouble. I nearly got shot by the cops, but I don't remember. My grandmother kicked me out, and I've got no-where to live."

"Yes, so, I'm to determine whether or not you're a danger to yourself. I understand you made a statement about wishing the police officer had 'pulled the trigger.' Is that true?"

"Yeah, I didn't mean it, though. You know, I was just feeling a little down, that's all."

Sneaking a peek at his wristwatch, he smiled and said, "I'm going to prescribe something for you, to help you relax. I'll make you an appointment to see me again in a month. In the meanwhile, try to remember that things are never as bad as they seem."

"Oh, really?" I said.

"Yes, really," he replied. "Not everything that happens to us can be blamed on others. You have the power to make decisions. Think about that. Tell Mary I'd like to see her for a moment, would you?"

I left his office actually thinking that maybe it was time to change my life. It was worth a try, things probably couldn't get worse.

# 5

# ENTERING THE RING

We returned to Mary's office, where I waited while she spoke with her supervisor. I wondered if they knew what to do with me. I dreaded the thought of another group home. If it came down to that I would grab my money and run.

"Great news, Tyler!" Mary gushed as she returned. "We've found you a place to stay. For now, anyway. It's an emergency foster home, a nice middle-aged couple; they used to foster full-time. And it's close to your school. So, let's get you home and settled in. Are you ready?"

"As I'll ever be," I said. "Do you think we could drop by my grandmother's first? I left something there that I'd really like to have, if it's not a problem."

"Well, Tyler, I hate to tell you this, I really do, but she . . . doesn't want to see you again. Maybe I could drop by tomorrow and get whatever it is that you need. Just tell me what to ask for. I really don't mind."

"It's okay. Forget it," I replied.

We drove to a quiet side street lined with neat-looking bungalows. The yards were all well kept, and the driveways were all paved. She pulled into number fifty-eight, shutting the car off and taking a deep breath.

"This will probably be only for a week or two, until we find you something more permanent. I think you'll like it here, Tyler. Mrs. Conway is a magnificent cook, and they're just wonderful people."

"Yeah," I said. I was nervous and just wanted to get inside and scope things out. As we got out and walked toward the side door, we had to pass between the house and the garage. Sunlight reflected off something behind the garage window as I walked by, jostling an old memory from back at my parents' house. I remembered the same thing happening as I passed by the garage there, but I had never checked it out. There was a hatchet hanging on the wall outside the door; Dad said it was for chopping my thumbs off if I ever went in there. I'd been so scared that I always walked by there sideways.

Mary rang the bell, and in seconds a smiling woman opened the door, wiping her hands on a flour-plastered apron. The aroma drifting out from behind her caused my mouth to water.

"Hello there, you must be Tyler!" she exclaimed. "Welcome to our home, young man. I was just throwing together some supper. *And* a little something to tide you over until then. I hope you like molasses cookies."

"Yes, ma'am, I do," I replied.

"Tyler, this is Mrs. Conway. Charlene, this is Tyler Josten," Mary said.

"Pleased to meet you, Mrs. Conway. And thank you for taking me in," I said.

"Oh my, think nothing of it, Tyler. We're glad to have you. We've got plenty of room, now that the kids have all grown up and moved on. Let's try those cookies."

I let Mary enter ahead of me, and we followed Mrs. Conway down the hall to the kitchen.

"Have a seat, you two, and I'll get the milk," Mrs. Conway said.

She piled a huge mound of cookies on a dinner plate and set it on the table. I had to swallow to stop from drooling. She placed a large glass of milk in front of each one of us and then sat down. The women talked and nibbled while I devoured five of the cookies.

"My husband will be home by dinnertime, Tyler. I called him at work and he's looking forward to meeting you," Mrs. Conway said. "Would you like to see your room now?"

"Sure," I replied. We went down to the basement, where there was a recreation room with a big-screen television. My new bedroom was tidy and clean, and the bed was huge.

"You have your own bathroom, Tyler, so you'll have lots of privacy. All I ask is that you keep it clean. If you'd like to have friends over, that'll be no problem, as long as they're out by ten o'clock. Wayne and I go to bed early. Is there anything else you need to know?"

"No, ma'am," I replied. "Thank you again for your hospitality, and the cookies were great."

"You're very welcome, Tyler, and please, call me Charlene," she said. "Let's get you settled."

It didn't take long to transfer my stuff to my room from the car, and I claimed that I felt like lying down for a while. I was exhausted from the tension of the last few days, and my nerves were jangled from trying *not* to think about what the future held for me.

I put my clothes in the dresser and stacked my books on top of it. I hung my shirts in the closet, which I noticed had no lock on the door. Then I lay down on the bed and quickly drifted off to sleep, trying not to think about the countless hours I'd spent locked in a dark, airless space.

***

I became aware of a gentle rapping sound, snapping awake when I realized someone was at my door. I got up and opened it to see a man who I assumed had to be Mr. Conway standing in the hall. He had scarred eyebrows and a dented nose, like someone you wouldn't mess with.

"Thought I'd come down and meet you before we ate — actually, to tell you that supper will be ready in about ten minutes. I'm Wayne. Pleased to meet you, Tyler, and welcome. Sorry to wake you up. I understand you had a bit of a rough spell," he said, offering his hand.

"I'm pleased to meet you, sir. I won't be any trouble, I want you to know that," I said, surprised that I actually seemed to mean it. I gave him a firm handshake, noticing that his forearms were knotted with muscle. His hand felt strong enough to crush mine.

"I don't expect you will be, son. See you upstairs in ten," he stated, then turned away.

# 6

# NEUTRAL CORNER

I washed up, tied my hair back, and went upstairs. I wasn't very comfortable in social settings and tended to just answer questions in as few words as possible. My main fear was that the meal might be a problem, that it might be something I couldn't bite into properly.

"Hope you like turkey!" chimed Charlene as I entered the kitchen. There were steaming mashed potatoes, peas, and beets, all arranged in the centre of the table in white serving bowls. In the middle of it all was a huge tray of turkey drumsticks, covered in some kind of sauce.

"Yes, ma'am. It smells delicious," I said.

"Dig in, Tyler, and don't be shy. Charlene can't get used to cooking small meals, and we've been throwing out enough leftovers to feed a small family. Our youngest just started college this year."

I filled my plate with the vegetables, then forked one drumstick onto the side. As soon as they'd filled their own plates, Wayne grabbed a drumstick and tore a huge bite off it. Charlene smiled and handed him some napkins as sauce dribbled down his chin. I used my knife to slice a piece of meat from mine, afraid that my teeth would hurt if I tried to bite it.

"So, Tyler, how do you like school?" asked Wayne.

"It's, uh, all right. I like history," I replied.

Wayne laughed and said, "That's a bad question. Not many guys your age actually like school, I guess. So, you like history, eh?"

"Yeah, especially war and stuff," I said.

"Well, you sure came to the right place,

Tyler, if you like to read about history and war. Go ahead, Wayne, I can see how excited you are," said Charlene with a proud smile.

"Well, I *do* happen to have a few books kicking around on those subjects. They're in my office downstairs. I'll show you after we do up the dishes. You're more than welcome to read them. That's what books are for, right?"

"Yes, sir," I replied.

We finished the main course, and Charlene started to clear the dishes. I stood up to help her, but she said to sit down and she'd have dessert on the table in a few minutes. Did I like coconut cream pie? Was this for real?

By the time we'd finished our pie I was as full as I could ever remember being. I was used to wieners and beans and microwave stuff, and as Wayne and I did the dishes I thought that I could get used to this pretty quickly.

"You interested in going for a drive, Tyler? I have to go down to the shop and see if a fax I've been waiting for has arrived yet. You may as well come with me. I'll show you the library when we get back."

"Well, yeah, okay," I said, wondering if he was afraid to leave Charlene alone with a juvenile criminal with a history of violence. Which was exactly what I was. We climbed into his pickup, and on the drive to the industrial park he explained to me what it was that he did. He owned a wood-working shop, making rafters and stairs and stuff for the construction industry.

We arrived at the industrial park and pulled up to the front of a huge warehouse. A sign on the front said "CW Fabricating — Done Right, On Time." I followed Wayne inside to his office, where he smiled as he removed a sheet of paper from the fax machine.

"All right," he said, "it looks like it's about to get busy around here. Come on, I'll show you the shop."

He hit a light switch on the wall beside a huge steel door and swung it open. We spent a half-hour wandering from machine to machine as he explained how each one worked, and also how each one could mangle you if you weren't careful. We climbed into the truck and headed back home.

"Man to man, Tyler, I want to tell you how welcome you are to stay with us, okay?" Wayne said as we pulled onto the street.

"Thank you," I said.

"We'll treat you with respect, so you do the same. Charlene's my main concern. You understand?"

"Yes, sir," I replied, fighting back anger. Still, I guess he had the right to tell me what he expected of me.

As soon as we got back to the house Charlene asked if we would like anything to eat.

"That's why I still work out, Tyler. If it was up to this gal, I'd weigh four hundred pounds, I swear," he said, putting his arm around her neck. I had a quick flash of my mom's face being forced downward in a headlock, and a muscular fist smashing into it. I had a thought that maybe Mom's behaviour, the booze, and the anger, wasn't entirely her fault. I blinked and shook my head to dislodge the image, but not before they saw the look on my face.

"Okay, let's check out those books," Wayne said.

The library was beautiful, with the walls done in some sort of pale golden wood, with hundreds of books arranged in shelves of the same material. In one corner of the room stood a stone fireplace and two antique-looking leather chairs, with reading lamps sitting on tables beside each one.

"Treat it like your own, son. A good book can take you far away, and we all need that once in a while, don't we? Let's grab a coffee and head for the garage. There's something you might be interested in."

# 7

## IN THE CLINCH

The first thing that I saw as we entered the garage was me, reflected in a wall that was mirrored from floor to ceiling. The other walls were covered in fight posters and pictures, and in the middle of the room stood a boxing ring. It had dark blue ropes, with bright red corner pads.

Wayne was smiling at me, and I knew that I should say something, anything, to please him. Some of the pictures on the walls resembled a younger version of him, and that gave me the break I needed.

"Wow. You boxed?" I said, hoping I

sounded impressed. I figured it couldn't be that hard, what with the gloves on your fists and a referee to save you when things got too rough.

"Yes, I did. Still do, actually. I still work out, and when I get the chance I go over to Shelburne and spar with the young fellows. They've got a great club there. In fact, one of their fighters won a silver medal in last year's nationals. Right now he's on a trip through Europe, with the national team. All expenses paid."

"What are all the pictures?" I inquired. "Some of them *are* you, right?"

"Yep, some of them are me, although a few years and a few pounds ago. See this one? It was just my third professional fight, against a guy with twenty-seven wins and four losses, twenty-one by knockout. Lucky I wasn't killed. It was scheduled for eight rounds, and I'd never been more than four. I got knocked down five times, had a broken nose and eleven stitches in my left eyelid, and lost by a country mile. But I finished the fight. Still, I should have known."

He stopped and seemed to be drifting back in his memory, reliving the sweat and punishment. I'd figured all boxers were tough-acting guys, and here was Wayne, about the nicest guy you could meet.

"Known what?" I asked.

"Known what was coming, Tyler. My manager wasn't the most ethical fellow you'd ever meet, to say the least. When he saw that I was a crowd-pleaser, that I would stand up and bleed, he threw me to the lions. I had six more fights and lost four of them, all by decision. All against fighters I had no business being in the ring with. Then I got smart and quit before I was permanently injured. My last fight, I was supposed to be paid four thousand dollars. I never saw a cent of it."

"What became of him, your manager?" I asked.

"Well, as they say, what goes around comes around. He got caught cheating in a card game in the back of a bar one night and was stabbed in the chest. He nearly bled to death and suffered brain damage from the lack of oxygen before they could get him to a hospital. He's in a nursing home now, hardly able to speak, so I guess he ended up like some of the poor guys he had fighting for him. Too bad, really."

It seemed to me that he'd only gotten what he deserved.

"But that's not real boxing, at least not the way it's meant to be. I had a barrel of fun fighting as an amateur and got to travel all over the world. Mexico, Russia, Ireland. It's a chance for a man to prove himself, *to* himself. Anyone can get in shape, learn the skills, but it's the mental aspect that's the real challenge. Even one fight, if a guy can overcome himself just that once, can change a life. It's all about confidence and self-respect. You can't buy that, you've got to earn it."

We went back into the house, and I went to my room after stopping to grab a book from the library. I picked one from the philosophy section, thinking that it would impress Wayne and Charlene. The problem was, after forty-five minutes I didn't have a clue what I'd just read.

There was a light tapping on my door and I opened it to find Charlene and Wayne standing in the hall.

"We're off to bed, Tyler. We'll see you in the morning. Do you need a ride to school?" Wayne asked.

"I'd rather walk, thank you," I replied, trying to look him in the eye.

"Well, we'll see you at breakfast, then," said Charlene, and before I knew what was happening, she stepped forward and gave me a quick hug. I froze like a stick, my arms hanging down limply as she let go, and Wayne saved the moment by clapping me on the shoulder and saying good night.

I lay back down and tried to remember if I'd ever had a hug before. I remembered watching Mom hug my little sister, and how it made my chest hurt with longing. My head filled with bad memories, and before I knew it I had myself in a rage. It was a long time before I fell asleep, and when my alarm sounded in the morning all I wanted to do was get high. The last thing I wanted was to face Wayne and Charlene and their happy, smiling world.

I faked my way through their cheery breakfast drivel and headed off to school. I told them that I might be a little late, there was something I had to do after school.

"Supper will be at six," Charlene said. "We'll see you then?"

"Yeah," I replied.

"Well, have a good day, son," Wayne said.

I'm not your son, I thought. By the time I arrived at school I'd cooled down a little, although my teeth were hurting like crazy, probably from gritting them in my sleep.

As I was leaning against the wall out back, waiting for the warning bell to tell me I had ten minutes until first class, Billy Turnbull and his gang approached me.

"Hey, Big Time. We heard you was shot

by the cops. You had a shootout with them or somethin'. What'd ya do, turn rat? You sure got out quick . . ."

That was as far as he got. I grabbed him by the throat and smashed him up against the brick wall. The look of fear in his eyes made me feel good.

"Talk to me again and I'll rip your windpipe out, you understand?" I said. "What did I just say?" I asked as he tried to choke out an apology. I jammed my left fist into his stomach, taking my hand off his throat and letting him fall to the pavement. Nobody made a move as I walked away.

The day went slowly by, and when the final bell rang I headed across town, sticking to the back streets. I arrived at Gram's house, and after making sure she wasn't home I forced open a basement window and slipped into the house.

# 8

## UPSTART

It was as dark as midnight down there. I stumbled around as I attempted to find the light switch. Cobwebs clung to my hair and face, and I became disoriented and started to panic. Finally I tripped over something, stumbling into the stairs that led to the pantry in the kitchen.

I wandered around the house, thinking that I was going to miss it there. I lay down on the couch and wondered what the next step in my life would be, after jail. Thinking of jail made me feel like running away, and that scared me as much as anything.

I got up and went to my bedroom, retrieving my money from the base of the table lamp and slipping back out of the house. With time to kill, I wandered down to the river and sat by the water. I had an idea in my head, something that I needed to talk to Wayne about.

After a while I headed home. I had twenty-two hundred dollars in my jacket pocket, and I imagined all the things I could buy if I wanted to. Still, I knew I wouldn't spend it. Depending on how things went with the cops, it might still be my ticket to freedom. It was a perfect fall afternoon, and as I walked I thought about apologizing for my behaviour at breakfast. Maybe the Conways hadn't even noticed. The house came into view, and I took a deep breath as I approached the door. I rang the bell twice and walked in.

"Hello! It's me, Tyler!" I called out. Both vehicles were in the driveway, so maybe they were outside somewhere. I hoped they weren't ignoring me because they were angry.

I rounded the corner into the kitchen. The

first thing I saw was a birthday cake and a gift sitting on the table. Charlene and Wayne were standing across the room, and they said, "Happy Birthday, Tyler," in unison.

After the bike fiasco when I was a kid, my parents had never mentioned my birthday again. Every year, like any kid, I hoped that someone would remember, but it never happened. I sat down, unsure of what to do.

"I know your birthday was yesterday, but we just found out today," Charlene said. "You should've told us, but better late than never, right?"

"Thank you. I didn't mention it because . . ." I began, but lost the thought. "Thank you very much."

I hoped they understood that I just didn't have it in me to be excited. I'd always survived by expecting the worst. You could only get hurt and disappointed by getting excited about the prospect of something good happening.

"I didn't cook supper, Tyler. We thought

you might enjoy going out for something," Charlene said. "Your choice. It's your birthday. But first, why don't we sample that cake? I'll get plates and forks. Grab me three glasses, would you, Wayne?"

We each had a slice of cake — a small one, so we didn't ruin our appetites — and a glass of milk. I was embarrassed about the gift, and hoped that I wasn't showing it. I was also getting a little curious about what was under that wrapping paper.

"Open it up, Tyler, see what you think," Wayne said as he slid the package across the table to me.

"Can I wait until later?" I asked.

"Sure, it's your gift," Wayne replied, as Charlene smiled like she understood.

"Okay, I'm going to lie down and read a bit. Whenever you guys feel like eating, just yell out to me," I said as I picked up the package and went downstairs.

I lay down on the bed and clutched the gift to my chest, and within minutes I was asleep.

That was all I wanted — to experience something good, just once, and to wake up to find it still there, still *real*.

I heard Wayne's voice calling my name, and I shook myself awake to find the gift still clamped tightly in my arms. The clock by my bed said six-thirty, and I realized that it wasn't morning but time to go out for supper.

"Can I come in?" he asked through the door.

"Sure," I replied, placing the present on my nightstand. I would've felt stupid having him see me holding it, as if it was really important to me. You never gave anyone that kind of power over you.

I stood up as he entered the room, and he pulled a bottle of pills from his shirt pocket. He cleared his throat as if he didn't know where to begin.

"Charlene picked these up earlier. It's what the doctor prescribed. Do you know what these are, what they're for?"

"Not really," I replied.

"They're downers, something to calm you down, if you need them. What they'll do is *slow* you down, rob you of your energy. It's none of my business, but I don't agree with trying to cure every damned thing that comes along in life with a pill. It's entirely up to you, though. Charlene will give you one every morning and evening, if you feel like you need them."

I thought of the fact that I hadn't had a toke for days, and how I'd become used to that mellowed-out feeling the weed gave me. Now I had a legal way to acquire the same feeling. I'd seen what people became like on these kinds of pills, and I didn't want to spend my days moving around in slow motion. Besides, that wouldn't fit with my plan.

"So, I can take them if I need them?" I asked.

"I guess so," he replied.

"I don't need them," I said. "I'll need to stay sharp from now on, Wayne."

He gave me a puzzled look, and I could tell

that he was anxious to hear what I was up to. I hoped he wouldn't laugh, as I took a deep breath, and a chance.

"I want to be a fighter," I said.

"I think you already are, Tyler."

# 9

# WARNING

We were waiting for Charlene to finish getting ready when Wayne mentioned a small problem with my plan. My heart dropped as I thought that maybe you couldn't compete if you had a criminal record.

"Charlene thinks it's barbaric," he said. "She never did get over seeing me look like I'd been truck-struck, and more than one time, too. She went to my first four professional fights, and after the fourth round of that one, she'd seen enough. That's the round where I'd got flattened twice, and I had a good cut over my left eye. So anyway, just keep it quiet for now. I'll talk to her about it, okay?"

"Yeah, okay," I said. It felt kind of sneaky, being asked to keep something from Charlene, and reminded me of how Dad had taught me to lie to Mom.

I'd always liked ravioli, or anything like that from a can, so I chose an Italian restaurant. We all had the linguine with clam sauce, which was delicious. It was also soft enough that I could eat without worrying about my teeth. By the time we'd left for home it was nearly bedtime, and I asked if I could wait until some other time to open my gift. They both seemed to understand, although I saw them exchange curious glances.

"Well, pleasant dreams," Charlene said. I tried not to flinch as she gave me a brief hug. Wayne followed me downstairs, where he told me that we could start working out the next evening.

"I don't know anything about boxing," I said.

"That's what I'm here for," he said, placing

his hand on my shoulder. I shuddered, and he quickly removed it.

"If you're serious, Tyler, you should get up a half-hour early and go for a run. You need to develop self-discipline. And not just for boxing. Run nice and easy, and when you get tired, walk until you get your breath back. Run a few blocks, and walk one. Go out six blocks or so, then come back. You'll be plenty tired by then. Once you recover, you'll be amazed at how alert you'll be all day. Oh yeah, just a glass of water before you run. If you eat you'll get sick. See you in the morning, man."

I slept holding my gift and wondered, as I was drifting off to sleep, how I'd ever be able to open it. I knew that I couldn't wait too long or I'd just end up looking ungrateful.

My alarm beeped at six-thirty, and I almost shut it off and went back to sleep. There was always tomorrow. Then I thought how bad it would look if I couldn't even perform my first workout. So I got up and was on the street in less than ten minutes, alone except for a lot of birds with a lot to sing about. I'd decided I would run four blocks and then walk two. I'd do it twice, then repeat it all over on the way back. *Not* a good plan.

After the first four blocks my legs were melting. I almost got my breath back during the walk, but by the time I'd run four more I was exhausted. I couldn't get enough air into my lungs, and my heart felt like it was hammering against my ribs. I collapsed on the grass next to the sidewalk, lying on my back as I concentrated on slowing my heart down.

"What's the problem?" I was startled to suddenly hear. My eyes popped open, and I found myself looking up the nostrils of two police officers. I clambered to my feet, and saw by their faces that it was going to be the good cop/bad cop routine. The younger guy was sneering, like he'd just discovered a pile of dog shit. The older guy with the beer belly was just blinking at me slowly from behind a sad-sack face.

"No problem at all, sir," I panted. "I was just out for a run."

"Yeah, right. Now tell me the truth," the young guy demanded.

"I'm staying with Wayne and Charlene Conway. I'm going to be a boxer. I'm doing road work." I explained between breaths. "It's my first run, and I guess I overdid it."

"Bullshit," he spat. "You remember me?"

"Yes, sir," I said, figuring he must've been one of the cops who'd arrested me.

"I know Wayne. Let's go see if your story holds up," the old cop said.

He opened the back door of the cruiser and I got in. As we pulled into the driveway I saw Wayne taking a newspaper out of the mailbox.

The young cop got out and swaggered toward the house but stopped when Wayne came walking toward him. He saw me sitting in the patrol car, and his face clouded with anger as he turned his gaze to the officer.

"Looks like Granville best mind his manners, uniform or not," said the older cop from the front seat. By Wayne's body language, it looked like he might be right.

Suddenly, as the cop was making a gesture like he might have been telling Wayne to relax, Wayne strode over to the car and opened the back door.

"Get out of there," he ordered.

I didn't hesitate, quickly springing from the seat. I'd just cleared the door when he slammed it. Hard. Then he opened the driver's door and said, "How's it going, Charlie?"

"Great, Wayne, just dandy. You?"

"Good, Charlie. Nice to see you again," he replied and then gently closed the door. He turned to the still-shocked-looking cop on the lawn.

"I would suggest you learn yourself some respect, boy," he said calmly. "Remember, it's not the uniform that makes the man. You have yourself a nice day."

Wayne looked at me and nodded toward the house, and I headed that way. As I reached for the doorknob, I looked back over Wayne's shoulder at the cop climbing into his car, looking like a whipped pup. The older guy was trying hard not to smile.

Once inside, Wayne acted like nothing at all had happened and asked me if I wanted eggs for breakfast. I went downstairs and had a shower while he cooked, and got back just as the toast popped up.

"How far did you get?" he asked.

"Ten blocks out," I replied.

He looked at me and smiled. "I see you listen as well as I do. Anyway, that was a good first run. You got anything big going on at school today?"

"No, sir," I answered. In my mind there was never anything important about school, on any day.

"How would you like to take the day off? We'll take a spin down to the shop, and I'll tell the boys they're on their own until tomorrow. You and I'll kick around for the day, do a workout this afternoon. I have some fight tapes I want to show you, too. What do you think?"

What did I think? I thought I'd like to quit school, kick around all day *every* day, and watch fight tapes.

"Sounds good to me," I replied. "Where's Mrs. Conway?"

"*Charlene*, Tyler," he said. "She left at six. Her mother's in a nursing home over in Milton. It's a two-hour drive, and she likes to get there early enough to help the nurses get her up and ready. She had a stroke. Her mind comes and goes, and most of the time she doesn't even know her own daughter. But Charlene still goes twice a week anyway. What can you do?"

*Forget about her*, I thought. I knew that if someday my mother or father or, better yet, both were in that position, that's what I would do.

# 10

## CAUGHT COLD

We finished eating, and after the dishes were washed and dried we climbed into Wayne's truck and headed for the shop. Wayne reached over and popped a disc into the player.

"Oldies," he chuckled. "Sorry."

He started singing along to the song that came on. By the time we'd arrived I was thinking that the song might be right. Maybe it never *was* too late to start all over again.

We went inside, and Wayne introduced me to the guys who worked for him. I tried my best to look them in the eye when we shook hands. A lifetime of keeping my eyes cast downward when I spoke to adults wasn't easy to overcome.

"Tyler's staying with us for a while," he said to the oldest guy, Bert, after the other two had returned to work.

"Great, hope to see you around," he said. "You'll be fine, son."

All of a sudden I was angry. When he said that I'd be fine, I thought that he knew too much about me, that maybe Wayne had been mouthing off. I'd always been aware of the pity people had for me, but that wasn't what I wanted. It wasn't what I needed. I realized that *now* I was looking Bert in the eye, with my teeth clenched and my breath coming in ragged gasps. He moved back a step.

Wayne read the situation quickly and said that we should be going. Bert pursed his lips and nodded, and I turned away, embarrassed. As I walked across the shop I thought about what Wayne had said about self-discipline. I turned back around.

"It was really nice to meet you, Bert," I said.

"Yeah, yeah, you too, Tyler. We'll be seeing you," he replied over his shoulder, looking puzzled.

Wayne and I drove home in silence. I snuck a peek at him, and he didn't look like he was angry or anything, more like he was thinking really hard. I hoped it wasn't about me, that he wasn't wondering if he really wanted me around.

Back at the house Wayne asked me if I wanted to watch a fight that he had recorded. He said it was the best fight he'd ever seen. He also said it would give me an idea of the level of skill and determination a person could achieve.

"Okay, here's a quick rundown on the fight," he began. "Roberto Duran's the white guy, he's from Panama, and he recently moved up to the welterweight class from lightweight. He'd been champ there for about seven years and beat everyone. This is his third fight at welterweight.

"The other guy is Sugar Ray Leonard. He won a gold medal in the Olympics in Montreal back in seventy-six. He's the champ and has skills most fighters can only dream about. The whole world was waiting for this fight, and it wasn't disappointed. Here goes."

On the screen the fighters answered the bell for the first round, and within seconds they were firing punches, hard and fast, both at the same time. By the end of the round I was amazed. And out of breath.

In the second round Leonard got hit by a shot that made his legs go wobbly, but he recovered quickly. They went back at it, winging non-stop punches from all angles for all fifteen rounds. The decision was announced, and Duran won. Leonard could hardly stand up or talk in the post-fight interview.

"Here we go again, the rematch, five months later," Wayne said. I admired Leonard's courage. It must've taken guts to face that guy again.

It was a totally different fight, with Leonard doing whatever he pleased and making Duran look like a fool. Suddenly, in the eighth round,

Duran threw his arms up and quit.

As he turned away from Leonard, who didn't know if it was a trick or not, he took a blistering left-right to the body and didn't even flinch. That pretty much ruined his story about quitting because he had stomach cramps.

"You know what happened, Tyler? Duran went home to Panama after the first fight and forgot what got him to the top of the sport. Self-discipline. He ate and partied, then couldn't get in shape quickly enough for the rematch. He was getting beaten and being made to look stupid, so he panicked and quit. That's his legacy — the tough guy who quit when the going got tough. Let's have some lunch, then you can watch me get beat up for eight rounds. Sound okay?"

"Yeah," I replied. What I *really* wanted to do was get a pair of boxing gloves onto my hands.

# 11

## IN THE FIGHT

We slapped together some turkey sandwiches and heated up a can of soup. I couldn't get past the feeling that Wayne wanted to tell me something, and the suspense was making me edgy. My instincts were right, because as we were putting our dishes into the sink he turned to me and cleared his throat.

"Charlene and I were thinking that if you wanted to, it's up to you, maybe you could stay here a while. I mean, as more than just an emergency thing. Anyway, think it over."

Something didn't feel right. I'd just arrived, and they didn't know me at all, and they were supposed to be done fostering.

"Um, sure," I said.

"Okay, we'll see what happens then. In the meantime, make yourself at home, and don't be shy about anything."

"Won't I be going to jail?" I asked. That was my big fear now, being locked up and losing my one chance to do something, well, special. To be somebody special. A fighter.

Wayne laughed. "You're not going to jail, Tyler. I can guarantee that. It was your first offence, and I know the system and everyone in it. We'll get you probation; you'll have a curfew and such. So just relax, that's that."

"Really?" I said. "For sure?"

"I wouldn't say it if I wasn't sure," he said. "Let's go watch that fight, then I have to get some vegetables ready for a stew. Then, if you want, we can do a workout."

My stomach flopped with excitement just thinking about it. We went back to the basement, and he started the fight. The bell sounded for the first round, and the fighters moved to the centre of the ring. Wayne immediately caught a double left hook, one to the body and one on the chin, and dropped flat on his butt.

"Smooth, eh?" he laughed, while on the screen the referee gave him the required eight-second count. Wayne didn't look too badly hurt, although maybe a bit embarrassed. When the ref waved the fighters back in, they both opened up and fired punches for about a minute before they fell into a clinch. The rest of the round was pretty tame, and Wayne gave almost as good as he got.

"Watch what he does when we're in close, Tyler. He keeps whacking me in the face with the side of his skull, trying to cut me. The referee never said a word, not even one warning. Here we go, round two."

The next two rounds went the same, with Wayne trying hard but getting hammered pretty well full-time. On the screen his face was starting to get puffy and red, and he was wincing every time the other guy ripped a shot to his body. It was about to get much worse.

"Okay, here comes the fourth round," Wayne said.

About halfway through the round his opponent blasted an uppercut through his guard, and followed with a straight right hand for the second knock-down of the fight. When Wayne got up, *really* slowly, there was blood pouring from his left eyebrow, and his legs wobbled as the ref finished the eight count. Within seconds he was flat on his back from another powerful combination, then got up just in time to beat the count. The ref asked him if he was all right, and he nodded yes. For the rest of the round he soaked up punches, and at the bell he staggered back to his corner.

"Watch, right there on the left of the screen. There goes Charlene, heading for the locker room. She always said that while she was waiting, her only hope was that I didn't come back on a stretcher."

The rest of the fight was one-sided, and Wayne hit the canvas twice more, but when the final bell rang, he threw his arms up in the air as if *he'd* won the fight. I knew that it was just pride in the fact that he'd showed the courage to keep going.

"So that was my first loss. What a mess I was — both my eyes swollen nearly shut and not a spot above my belt that wasn't bruised. It hurt even to blink. But I was proud because I'd survived, and the crowd gave me a bigger ovation than they gave him. I should've quit right there, but I still had dreams. Anyway, you ready?"

I wanted to tell him how much I admired his courage, but it didn't seem like it would mean much coming from a kid. Still, I knew what it was like to face a sure beating and not run from it. We had that much in common.

It took us an hour to prepare the vegetables, and we talked the whole time, or at least Wayne did. It was the first time I'd ever had a normal conversation with an adult.

"Yeah," he said, "life is like boxing in a lot of ways. Once you're born, the bell has rung, and you're in the fight. You can run, you can quit, or you can keep swinging and get up every time you get knocked down. We all have that within us, Tyler, that inner strength. The biggest mistake you can make is to let anyone take it away from you. By overcoming, you gain strength. Never forget that."

We cleaned up our mess, put the stew on to simmer, and went out to the garage. I had no work-out clothes, but Wayne said we could take care of that after supper.

He handed me a pair of black leather gloves, about as thick as insulated winter mittens, and I slipped them on.

"We'll start out on the focus pads, get you used to the basic punches before you hit the heavy bag. Relax, it takes practice, so don't get frustrated. This is the most important step. Any mistakes you learn here will stay with you. Now, watch me, and try these punches out, there in the mirror."

He showed me the jab, and the straight right hand, which in my case was the straight left, since I was left-handed. And how to pivot my shoulder for a hooking punch. I felt a little stupid, being so awkward, but I didn't get frustrated or embarrassed or angry. After he figured I had a pretty good understanding of those basic punches, he slipped on the focus mitts.

They were big flat leather pads, about two inches thick, the size of dinner plates. They had fingerless gloves sewn on the back. When he put them on and held them up, they became two targets, complete with red bull's eyes in the centre.

"Okay, let's get in the ring and give it a go," he said.

# SUCKER PUNCH

I started out throwing jabs, since that was the first punch he'd shown me, then started following them with the straight left. Every once in a while he'd turn one pad sideways, which presented a target for the hook. It was really difficult, because every time he moved his body, I had to adjust my feet, and a few times I nearly tripped.

"There you go, that's your first round," he said, nodding to the big clock on the wall. "You did great. Just remember to turn your fist over on the straight punches and stay loose. Breathe deeply, this is about the quickest minute you'll ever know."

He wasn't kidding. We went back to it, and I kept pumping the jab, and smacking my left dead centre on that bull's eye. Wayne would reward any good shots, the ones that made a sharp cracking sound, with a nod of his head. After three rounds we stopped for a break, and when I'd caught my breath I asked him when we'd be sparring.

"In a few weeks," he said. "There's no sense in it until you get your feet under you and build up some endurance. You won't believe how tired you'll get from just one round of it. You'll think your legs have turned to rubber. Same thing with the heavy bag — there's no sense in trying for power until you've got the mechanics of punching under control. Let's do two more rounds, then I'll get you started on the speed bag."

The first one went smoothly enough. In the second round he started holding the pad on his left hand against his cheek, on its edge, so that it was just like another face right beside his. As the round was winding down, he said, "Nail that," shaking the pad to indicate which one he meant. "Step right into it. Relax, stay loose, make it fun."

It was fun, until I messed up.

I let one fly and could tell by the look he gave me that I'd impressed him. He moved off to my right, and I followed him, ripping a shot with everything I had left.

My legs were tired, and as I pivoted to throw the punch I lost my balance. The shot hit him flush in the mouth, and he tore off one pad and threw his hand up to his face. I barely had time to react before he brought it back down, and I braced myself for a return punch.

Instead of hitting me, he smiled, and where his four top front teeth had been was a huge gap. Before I realized there should have been blood, he held up the teeth, which were false. The look on my face must have been funny, because he burst out laughing.

I tore off the gloves, threw them to the floor, and headed for the door. He was no different than anybody else. He'd been waiting for a chance to make me look stupid.

As I reached for the doorknob he stepped by me, putting his hand against the door so I couldn't open it. I gave it a good tug anyway, but it didn't budge. Turning my head to look at him, I saw that instead of being mad, he looked like I'd hurt his feelings.

"Don't be swinging at shadows, Tyler," he said. "This is a new day. It was just a joke. I didn't mean any harm."

"I'm sorry," I forced myself to say.

"Don't worry about it. You're angry, I can see that. You probably have reason to be. Anger will eat you up if you don't channel it properly. I'm not going to tell you *not* to be angry, just to learn to control your anger, instead of letting it control you. Hey, what's a punch in the mouth between friends, anyway? Let's try out that speed bag."

He showed me how to hit the bag, first with the back of one hand, then with the face of the other fist. Then you hit it with the back of that fist, then the face of the *other* fist. Over and over, or at least in his case. I tried it, and could see that it would be a tricky skill to learn. I had a hard time hitting it twice in a row before it bounced off in whatever direction it wanted.

"Follow the sound. You have to look at the bag, of course," he explained, "but it's too fast to hit by sight. The sound will give you the rhythm. I'll leave you alone. I'd better check on supper."

I flailed away until I couldn't hold my arms up anymore, but I was pleased at how quickly I was picking it up. I went for a shower and then lay down to read until it was time to eat, feeling like my first workout had gone well. Except for punching Wayne in the face.

There was a tap on my bedroom door, and Wayne said that supper was ready. I ladled a big helping of stew into a bowl and joined him at the table. There was homemade bread stacked in thick slices on a plate and a pitcher of milk beside it. I'd never eaten so well before and imagined that, being in training,

I would be putting on some muscle pretty quickly. I liked the sound of that. *In training.*

"This is good stew," I managed to say through a mouthful of whole-wheat bread.

"More like vegetable soup," he chuckled in reply. "We forgot the main ingredient, the meat."

"We?" I replied.

Wayne kept glancing over at me, like he wanted to say something but didn't know how to go about it. I was starting to get uncomfortable when he finally spoke.

"Tyler," he finally said, "it's really none of my business, I guess, but could you tell me why you're not opening your birthday present?"

I took a deep breath, and for whatever reason decided to just tell him the truth. Maybe *this* was a good time to start all over again.

"It's the first gift I've gotten since I was seven," I began, wishing I could look him in the eye. "That year I got a bike. Brand new — shiny chrome and blue paint. My dad didn't like me much, he was pretty rough, but I figured it was the start of a new life. That lasted about ten minutes, and then it was gone. Everything, I mean — the fantasy of a new life, *and* the gift. So I guess maybe . . . I don't know, I just think it's safer *not* to open it, I guess. Is that stupid?"

"No, no, not at all," he said, "I'm sorry to hear that, Tyler. I don't know what to say. That gift, it was Charlene's idea. It's yours, Tyler, and it'll stay yours. I know it's not easy, but the past is just that, *the past*. This is now."

We heard the door open, and Charlene breezed into the kitchen, catching us both by surprise and shutting the conversation down. Wayne got up and gave her a hug, asking her how the day had gone. Her mother had been pretty good, she said, and they'd even gone to the park for a stroll.

"What's up with you guys? What happened to your lip, Wayne?"

"I was showing Tyler how to hit the pads, and he hit me instead. No big deal. A little swelling, that's all."

"I'm going to be a fighter. Wayne's going to train me," I blurted, forgetting that he was supposed to break it to her. It was just that I wanted to change the subject quickly. I didn't really want to share the birthday story with her.

"Uh, I guess I'm ready to open my present now," I said. "I'll be right back."

## COVERING UP

Returning to the kitchen with the gift under my arm, I heard Charlene harshly whispering something to Wayne. I hoped he wasn't in trouble about the boxing thing. I set the package on the table and started to tear it open, but Charlene said, "The card first, Tyler. Open it first, please?"

So I opened it. The scene on the front of the card was of a mountain, high in the clouds, backed by a sunbeam-streaked sky. Inside was a sappy poem in fancy script about climbing your personal mountain. It was inscribed, *Welcome to our home, Tyler.*

A few days before, I'd been kicked out of a house that wasn't a home anyway. I had no friends, or even family, and no plans for the future except maybe running away somewhere. It was almost too much. I couldn't find anything to say, so I was really glad about having to open the gift, because it gave me an escape route.

I tore open the gold wrapping paper, exposing the box inside. I lifted the top, and there it was, a black leather jacket. I unfolded it and slipped it on; it fit as snugly and sleekly as a second skin.

"Thank you," I said.

"It fits you well," Charlene said.

"Um, can I go now, to my room?" I asked.

"Sure," Wayne said.

Back in my room I hung the jacket on my chair, so I could see it from the bed, and lay down. I had this ability that I'd developed when I was a kid, where I could completely shut down anything that I didn't want to think about. It was some kind of protective instinct that I had developed. When I was told that

Dad was going to straighten me out when he got home, I'd freeze up with fear. Then I'd do everything wrong, and get more and more frightened of his arrival, until I couldn't even breathe properly. I would've gone crazy if I hadn't found a way to control it.

Although this was different, it was still too much to handle. I'd only ever dealt with fear and hate and guilt and anger. I had no idea how to deal with whatever this was. I wanted to get high.

As I lay there admiring the jacket I thought about the kids at school, who would probably think that I'd stolen it. That got me thinking about things that I'd had stolen from me over the years. Like the returnable bottles that I'd collected and left stored under the porch, only to find them gone one morning.

Or the tape measure that I'd sneaked from the basement and taken to school. I had wanted the other kids to think my dad let me use his stuff. I remembered the horror of discovering that it was no longer in my desk after lunch hour one day. Stolen by some kid jealous of my fantasy relationship with my father.

Or my bike. No matter what the lesson was supposed to have been, it was still a theft, and it had been a lot more than blue paint and chrome stolen that day.

I ended up falling asleep and dreamed that Dad was carrying me upstairs, dangling by my wrist from his hand while I yelled again and again, "I want my bike back!" It went on and on, and in the dream I knew that the stairs had no end.

There were three loud knocks on my bedroom door, and I sprung to my feet beside the bed as I heard Wayne's voice.

"You okay, Tyler?" he said. "It sounded like you were having a nightmare."

"No, I'm fine. I mean, yeah, I was having a weird dream, but no, I'm fine," I said.

"If you'd like, why don't we go get you some work-out clothes?"

"Uh, all right, yeah. I'll be up in a few minutes," I answered.

I washed my face and retied my hair. I wondered if I should get it cut short if I was going to be a fighter. I put on my jacket and joined Wayne and Charlene upstairs. Wayne showed me a workout schedule that he'd put together for me. He saw the look on my face and guessed what it was about.

"Noticed the skipping, eh?" he laughed. "It's not little-girl skipping, you know. Every fighter does it. It's tremendous for putting spring into your footwork. I still do it. I'll show you how."

There was a book lying face down by his elbow, and when he saw me glance at it he passed it over. It was *The Art of War* by Sun Tzu, some ancient Chinese general.

"If you get time, read that," said Wayne. "It's got a lot to teach anyone about *any* type of combat, especially the mental aspect. Winning smart is easier than winning tough."

At the mall we found sweatsuits that fit me, and I grabbed two of them. As we stood in the checkout line Wayne started fidgeting, and as we got closer to the cashier he got worse. Finally, when there was one customer left between us and the checkout girl, he said, "Um, here, I'll get those," reaching for the outfits.

"I'll get them," I replied, and stepped forward to pay for them with the money I'd brought. If he was shocked to see me hand the two fifty-dollar bills to the girl, he didn't show it.

Back at the house, I tolerated another bedtime hug from Charlene. I guess it made her happy. I fell asleep reading *The Art of War*. If Wayne thought reading it would increase my chances of succeeding, then I'd *study* it. I was in too deep now and just *couldn't* fail.

# GLASS JAW

I awoke to the sound of a driving rain. I knew that if nothing was going to stop me from succeeding, then a little rain *was* nothing. So I ran. I returned home soaked to the hide, where Charlene met me at the door.

"I started filling the tub with hot water as soon as I realized where you'd gone. Get down there and soak the chill out. Breakfast will be in about half an hour," she said sternly. "Honestly, *men*."

Wayne was finished eating by the time I arrived upstairs, and he was preparing to leave for work. He said he had to hurry but that

Charlene would drive me to school later. I tried to protest, but they'd have none of it.

"Okay, I'm off," Wayne said. He kissed Charlene goodbye, grabbed a lunch box and Thermos off the counter on his way out, and left us alone.

"There's lots of time before we have to leave. Would you like a cup of hot chocolate?" she asked.

"Um, okay," I replied, even though I didn't want one. "I'll get my stuff."

I gathered my things for school, and before I went back up to the kitchen I stopped to brush my teeth. I pushed my lip up and took a look at my gums, seeing that they were purple and swollen. I had no idea how much a dentist would cost, but it looked like I was going to have to find out, and soon.

"Smells good," I lied as I returned to the kitchen.

"Yes, it does, it smells wonderful. It certainly does," Charlene replied. I knew that she had something to discuss other than how good the hot chocolate smelled. My stomach had done the flip-flop that always warned me when something was up.

"Wayne and I were speaking last night, Tyler, about this . . . thing," she began.

*I should've known,* I thought.

"We really hope you'll stay with us," she continued. "Anyway, as a foster child, Family Services will pay to have your teeth fixed. Although we don't care, we'll pay for them. It's not an issue. Oh goodness, what I'm trying to say is this: if you want to get your teeth fixed, now would be a good time. We just wanted you to know that."

She put her head down and exhaled loudly, like she was as embarrassed as I was. Even though they'd never seen me smile, I guess they knew I had dental problems from having watched me eat. All I could think was, *don't get angry*. She was just being kind.

"I've been thinking about that lately," I said. "You know, about seeing a dentist."

"I'll make you an appointment today," she said.

I usually had no problem finding something to daydream about in class. My whole life had changed during the last week. Even though I knew things could go to pieces quickly, I was going to enjoy it while I could. It was the first time that I'd truly felt safe. And safe to dream.

The week flew by and suddenly it was Friday. Dentist day. Running in the mornings, school all day, homework, and then working out in the evenings. The days disappeared like smoke on a breeze. I was getting sharp really quickly and could land four or five good, flat punches in a row on the pads. Wayne was impressed, and I guess I was too.

I was nervous all day, and a few times I thought about skipping out on school and missing my dentist's appointment. The only thing that stopped me was the thought that Wayne might think I was a coward. So I handed in my note at the office and waited in front of the school for him to pick me up.

The dentist turned out to be a nice guy (I was learning that most people were actually nice) and he explained everything to me as he went along. None of it helped to relax me. Finally it was over, and I had four new fillings.

I went into the washroom where I scrubbed the crud from the drill off my face and rinsed my mouth out with some spearmint stuff. As I was heading for the front desk to have my next appointment made, I heard Wayne's voice. I stopped and listened.

". . . a natural. I've never seen anyone run off combinations like that before, Carl, I'm serious, after only a few days. I tell him something, and he does it. He ran in that freezing rain the other day, that's how serious he is. And he's far from stupid. Reads stuff I don't, or, I should say, can't. Charlene just loves him. Anyway, he's had it real rough, you can see it in his eyes, but he'll be fine. I'd better scoot, he's probably waiting for me out front. See you soon."

"All right, Wayne, I'll make sure I go see him fight, and don't forget, you're overdue for your yearly. About a year overdue, actually."

I made it just in time to be standing in front of the desk when he came out, where the receptionist gave me a little card with the date of my next appointment on it. I felt like an idiot, mumbling thank you to her, and then wiping the drool off my chin.

# 15

## SPLIT DECISION

My mouth was so numb that the better part of the drink of water I took when I got home dribbled down my chin. I couldn't eat because I was afraid I'd mess up the fillings, or worse, end up chewing on my tongue and not knowing it.

We did a workout, and I tried extra hard to keep Wayne impressed with my progress. I stayed really loose and relaxed, so that the punches were smooth and fast. I finally managed to skip for a whole minute without the rope attacking my ankles, and he got me started on abdominal exercises. I'd never imagined there was so much work involved in being a boxer. And weightlifting, sparring, and the heavy bag weren't even a part of my routine yet. I finished by doing fifteen minutes on the speed bag, then hit the shower.

The book Wayne had given me was really interesting. If you applied what it said to ring combat, it looked like deception was the key to victory. In fact, it said that "All warfare is based on deception." If the enemy couldn't figure out what you were up to, he'd lose heart and then the fight. Kind of like when Wayne showed me how to pretend I was throwing one punch, when actually I'd be throwing something completely different.

It reminded me of Dad, of how I'd never known what he was thinking or how he would react to something I did. So I'd always been bewildered and frightened of what would happen next and couldn't function properly.

On Saturday I spent the day reading and watching fight films from Wayne's collection, stopping the action to try out some of the moves I saw in front of my mirror. Wayne and Charlene had gone to visit friends, and I was bored, wishing I had some weed.

Sunday morning they went to church. They invited me along, but I said I needed to work on an essay for English class. As soon as they'd left I called a cab and went to my dealer's place, then ran back home with two grams of skunk weed in my pocket. I got high out behind the garage, then went to work on my essay. Mr. Breen had said we could pick the subject, as long as it was at least a thousand words, and I went into a weed-inspired frenzy of writing.

In half an hour I had fifteen hundred words on the importance of goals in life. I figured I had plenty of time, so I smoked another joint. I went into the garage, just to be around the boxing equipment. Within minutes the Conways' car pulled into the driveway, and I watched out the garage window in horror as Wayne noticed the light on inside. He turned and walked toward me, Charlene right behind him. I had nowhere to run, and I knew that I stunk of weed.

"Smells like skunk out here," I heard Wayne say as he held the door for Charlene.

She looked at me as she stepped inside, and I could tell that she knew I was high. She turned and brushed past Wayne, leaving the door open behind her.

Wayne watched her go, then slammed the door shut, making me jump. I could see the anger in his eyes as he walked toward me.

"You're high," he said.

"What?" I said. "No."

"Don't lie to me, Tyler," he said calmly. "Are you high?"

"No," I said. He sighed.

"Your eyes are red and glassy, and you look like you're about to fall asleep," he said. "It smells like a skunk sprayed in here. Look at me when I'm speaking to you."

"I can't," I said.

"And why is that, Tyler?" he said.

"I don't know!" I yelled.

"Yeah, you know," he said. "You were beaten down your whole life, taught that you were worthless by someone who thrived on the weakness they instilled in you. You have no respect for yourself, and it transfers to everyone else. That's why. Do you want to be a fighter?"

"Yes," I said.

"Then be a fighter," he said, turning to the door.

"I can stay?" I asked as he pulled it open.

"That's your decision," he said.

I went directly into the house, downstairs to my bathroom, and washed the weed residue off myself. Then I flushed the weed down the toilet, put on my sweats, tied my hair back, and headed out for a run. Charlene was in the kitchen as I passed through, standing at the sink.

"I'm very sorry, Charlene," I said. "If you guys will have me, I want to stay."

"I'm glad, Tyler," she said, drying her hands. She walked over to me as I studied my laces, putting her arms around me, giving me a gentle squeeze. I hustled out the door as she released me. I didn't want her to see me cry.

I never cried. I couldn't. It was the one thing that I wouldn't give up. I remembered Dad laughing when I cried, telling me what a weakling I was.

"Men don't cry," he would say. "So what does that make you?"

I ran, trying to blink back tears, turning the hurt to anger. My hair bouncing on my shoulders reminded me of the last time Dad had made me cry. It was when he had said that if I was a girl, I was going to need a girl's hair. I thought about beating his face to a pulp with my fists.

# 16

## STABLEMATE

On Monday morning, on the way to my locker, I walked by a group of guys milling around the water fountain. I heard someone say something about my jacket, and they all laughed. They should have known better.

I kept walking. I handed in my essay at the beginning of first-period English, and after class Mr. Breen asked if he could have a word with me.

"This is excellent," he said, holding up my essay. "I read it during class. I wanted to tell you that if you can produce work like this, well, keep doing it. There's no pride in *not* trying, Tyler."

"I know," I said.

At lunch I went to the cafeteria, taking my usual seat alone in the back corner, next to the hallway. I'd just started eating when I heard a voice beside me.

"Me sit you?"

I turned to see Joey Dalton standing there, a hopeful smile on his dopey face. I'd noticed him watching me lately and had figured it wouldn't be too long until he approached me. I assumed that took courage, because I knew that a lot of people weren't very kind to him. Maybe they thought it was his fault that he'd been born with Down's syndrome.

"Sure, Joey, sit right down. What's up?" I replied.

"Tuna," he answered. "A lotta tuna."

I tried to think of something to talk to him about as he tore into his sandwich, fish and bread crumbs raining off his chin. Before I could come up with anything, a ruckus started in the hallway behind me. I heard a voice say, "Hey, it's the 'tard. I bet he's got some goodies for us again."

I swivelled my head around to see who it was while Joey squealed and leaned forward, his arms cuddling his lunch. I stood up just as three guys rounded the corner, the smiles falling from their faces when they saw me. They quickly took off, but I'd seen who they were.

"They won't bother you again, okay?" I said.

"You friend?" he asked.

"Yeah, I guess," I said. "You eat lunch with me from now on, okay?"

"'Kay!" he said and offered me his hand. I shook it, then casually reached down and wiped the mayonnaise and tuna off my hand onto the bottom of my chair.

I sat there watching him eat and wondered what it must be like for him. I wondered if he knew he was different. Or maybe he just thought everyone else was different.

It dawned on me that there wasn't much

difference between the two of us, except the obvious one, of course. We were both misfits, loners, although I actually had a choice in the matter, while Joey didn't.

I came home from school Thursday afternoon to find Wayne and Charlene waiting at the kitchen table. I could tell there was something wrong as soon as I saw their faces. I barely had time to accept that they'd changed their minds about me when Wayne spoke.

"The police were here, Tyler," he started. I barely heard the rest of what he said, I was so relieved that it was just the cops. I was looking forward to getting the whole affair over with.

". . . down to the station later this evening," he concluded.

"Okay, good," I said. "Are you coming?"

"I'll be there, Tyler," he said.

"What do you think?" I asked.

"It's an impressive list, for sure, but they always break things into as many separate charges as they can," Wayne said. "The judge will look at the whole thing as one event, and you've got no previous record, so your pre-sentence report will be favourable. Charlene and I will stand behind you, of course. We'll talk to some people. Everything will be fine — you'll get probation. Are you okay? You look a little shocked."

"No, I'm fine," I replied.

"Are you boys going to work out before supper or wait until later?" Charlene asked, dismissing the subject.

We decided to do it before supper, and I quickly got lost in the intensity of honing my skills. *Warrior skills*. I loved the sound of that in my head. I was slipping the gloves on to hit the speed bag when Wayne casually asked me a question.

"Did you ever have that gun out before the night you were arrested?"

"No, sir, never," I answered.

"All right, I'll see you inside," he said. I wondered why he'd asked me about the gun. People didn't ask questions without a reason.

After supper Wayne and I washed and dried the dishes like we usually did, which was only fair seeing as how Charlene did the cooking. He said we'd leave for the police station in about an hour, so I went to my room to read for a while. I was still enjoying *The Art of War*, especially the stuff about outmanoeuvring the enemy. It seemed natural to me, and I wondered if maybe being a fighter was what I had been meant to be.

"You ready, Tyler?" Wayne shouted from the top of the stairs. My stomach lurched, but I reminded myself that everything was fine. The cops were only going to ask a bunch of questions, and it wasn't that big of a deal. I was trusting Wayne on this one.

# 17

# TECHNICAL DECISION

Charlene walked to the door with us and, of course, gave me a hug. I tried to respond but couldn't move my arms. Wayne tried to make small talk on the way into town, but I just grunted responses. He announced us at the desk, and we took a seat on a bench and waited.

"Oh, by the way, I picked you up a mouth-piece today," Wayne said. "We'll start sparring on Monday, if you like."

My stomach flopped with excitement. I'd *really* be on my way to being a fighter. You could run, lift weights, and hit all the bags that you wanted to, but to be a fighter, you had to *fight*.

"You can go in now. Second room on your left," the guy behind the desk said, nodding to indicate a metal door in the corner of the waiting area. A buzzer sounded as we approached, and Wayne pulled the door open for me. I jumped as it swung shut with a final-sounding clack of metal behind us. That was when the butterflies really started up in my stomach.

It was the officer who'd driven me home the morning of my first run. The same guy who had his gun on me the night I messed up. Constable Granville, his name tag said. He seemed really pleasant this time, almost shy when he looked at Wayne.

He read me my rights and told me that I could have a lawyer present if I wanted. He asked me if I understood the charges as he read them to me, and I told him that I did. Then he asked me if there was anything I wanted to add.

"No sir," I replied.

He gave me a tight smile and said, "Now, about the marijuana, Tyler. If you could provide us with the name of the individual who sold it to you, we might be able to help you out on a few of the other pending charges. How do you feel about that?"

"No," Wayne said.

"Tyler?" Granville asked.

"No," I said, not sure what *pending* meant.

"Approximately two weeks before the incident involving Tyler and the gun, there was an armed robbery at a convenience store near where he was then residing," Granville said. "The perpetrator wore a mask, but the description given to us by the clerk on duty that night fits him well. The security-camera footage indicates the same. Would you like to tell us anything else, Tyler?"

That was why Wayne had asked me about the gun. He thought that I might have pulled an armed robbery. And he'd seen me with that money at the mall. I guess I couldn't blame him for suspecting me.

"No, sir," I replied. "The first time I ever had that gun out was the night you guys arrested me, I swear."

I knew that by not making eye contact with Granville it probably looked like I had something to hide. I also knew that the police couldn't charge me without better proof than they had. Or could they?

"Well, as luck would have it," the cop continued, "the robber left us some fingerprints on a soft-drink bottle that he moved out of his way while he emptied the till. If you were to agree to be printed, we could possibly eliminate you as a suspect. I mean, since you claim no involvement in the matter. What do you think about that, Tyler?"

"No problem," I told him. "I'd be glad to prove that it wasn't me."

"Any objections to that, Mr. Conway?" he asked Wayne.

"Not if Tyler agrees, no," he answered.

"All right, if you gentlemen would follow me, we can get this over with quickly," the cop said.

We went up the stairs to the fingerprinting room, a cramped little space with dull grey walls. I imagined how it would feel to be in there if you were guilty, and about to have it proven, instead of being about to be cleared, like me.

My breath caught in my throat, and my whole body went numb as Granville looked at me and said sternly, "Give me your hand."

In my mind I saw myself as a little kid, choking in a headlock while my fingers were pressed onto the red-hot burner of a stove. I took a deep breath and shuddered.

"Your hand, give me your hand," the cop repeated. I held out my right hand, and he rolled each finger on an ink pad, then onto a piece of paper.

"Now the left," he said, seeing my hesitation. He smiled, one of those "gotcha" smiles. He repeated the process, looking puzzled when the index finger registered no print. Same with the middle, then the ring finger. I let him try again.

"What the hell is this?" he asked.

"I'll tell you what the *hell* it is," I said. "I was eight. My little sister stole money from my old man's pocket while he was passed out drunk. My old man blamed me. For stealing, and lying about it, he held my fingers on a stove burner. I was *eight* years old."

"Okay, we're done here," Wayne said.

"We'll be done when I say we're done!" I yelled. Then I felt stupid, because we *were* done.

"We'll be in touch," Granville said, grimacing like he'd slammed his fingers in a door. As we crossed the parking lot I told Wayne I would walk home.

"Okay," he said.

I was cutting through back streets, trying to shorten the walk home, when I saw two guys standing outside a pool hall.

"Hey, faggot!" one of them yelled. I stopped and turned to face them.

"You girls got a problem?" I asked. They looked at me, then at each other, like they couldn't believe their luck. They were both a lot bigger than me, and older.

"It ain't us that got the problem," one of them said as they started across the pavement toward me. "It's you's got the problem."

I stood really still and watched them approach, so wired with excitement that I felt like giggling. They stopped right in front of me, both of them smirking. I whipped a jab flush onto one guy's chin, connecting solidly. His eyes rolled and he dropped, and before he hit the pavement his friend was on his knees spitting teeth into his left hand. I walked away.

I still had a long way to go to get home. I walked and jogged until I reached the bridge that crossed the Cleeland River. I was five minutes from home, so I crawled over the railing and sat down on an abutment to think things over.

The lights on the bridge behind me shone in streaks across the black water below, and the rippling pattern of darkness and light was mesmerizing. I imagined how quickly the cold water would swallow me up, and the only people who would care were Charlene and Wayne. Strangers.

I climbed back over the railing and walked home. When I arrived the house was dark, except for the hall light. Taped to my bedroom door was a note, in Charlene's handwriting.

*Welcome home*, it said. I didn't cry.

# TRADING PUNCHES

The next morning I was up ahead of my alarm. I stepped outside into the crisp morning air and ran for my life. I ran away from everything that had come before, and toward whatever was ahead. I ran until I couldn't run anymore, then I ran some more. The wind in my hair and the breath in my lungs made me feel like I could fly. I returned home higher than I'd ever been.

I was tense with excitement all day at school as I thought about sparring for the first time.

When I got home Charlene told me that

Wayne had called, and that he'd be a few hours late. The police had called also, confirming that the fingerprints at the crime scene couldn't have been mine. I wondered if Charlene had thought I was capable of armed robbery, but didn't ask. I ate at five, then paced, and read, and paced some more until I heard the truck pull into the driveway.

"Ready for battle?" Wayne said.

"All my life, yeah," I told him.

"I'll be out in five minutes," he said.

We shadowboxed two rounds to loosen up, and then put on the padded leather headgear and sixteen-ounce sparring gloves. They felt as big as pillows, and when I put my hands up they nearly blocked my view.

"Just relax and remember what I've told you," Wayne said, tapping the electric timer with his glove. "We'll start in ten seconds."

The timer buzzed and he nodded, putting his hands up and sliding toward me. I moved out of my corner to meet him, and he threw a jab at my face. It was an easy one, and I slipped my head to the side and countered with a right hook to the body, which he caught with his elbow. I immediately brought my glove back up to protect my jaw, and he whacked it with a light left hook.

I was so nervous that I couldn't stop flinching every time Wayne made a move. He started pressing me, forcing me to keep moving. I tried to throw punches but couldn't keep my balance. He kept snapping punches at me, and before long I was out of breath. My legs refused to do what I wanted, and when the buzzer sounded I was so exhausted that I flopped to the floor.

As I lay there fighting to get my breath back, he began telling me things that I'd done wrong, and a few things that I'd done right. He wasn't even breathing hard.

Wayne let me recover for two minutes, and then we did another round. He spent most of the round covering up on the ropes, hiding behind his gloves. When I'd open up on him he'd counterpunch me with light, well-placed shots. Near the middle of the round, he popped me with a solid right hand flush in the face, and I nailed him with a straight left to the body in return. He smiled and nodded.

I figured the round was drawing to a close, so I opened up, firing punches non-stop until he locked me in a clinch when the buzzer sounded. I stayed on my feet during the break, and the third round was a sloppy mess, at least for me. By the time it ended I felt like I might puke.

"You did well, Tyler. You've got the instinct, and now you know the secret, right?"

"Huh?" I managed to say.

"You have to relax and stay loose. Wait until your first fight, you'll see what I mean," Wayne said.

After I recovered somewhat, he got me to shadowbox one round to keep my muscles loose. My hands were so light without the pillow gloves on that they seemed to move in blurs. I practised the moves that had worked in combat, and Wayne gave me tips on what I could do to improve them.

He wrapped my hands for me, and I moved to the heavy bag. The bag gloves were lighter than the sparring gloves, and the padding was flat and solid. Wayne gave me instructions as I planted my feet and ripped combinations into the bag. The smack of leather on leather was like music to my ears. I did two rounds before my muscles just quit. Another round of shadowboxing was followed by abdominal work, and then it was time for a shower. I felt like a warrior.

# 19

# FRINGE CONTENDER

Another week went by in a blur of activity. I lived to spar now, trading punches with Wayne like I was born to it, even enjoying it when I got hit. The excitement of training for my first fight was the best buzz I'd ever felt.

I still kept to myself at school, except for lunchtime with Joey. It was a bother, but I figured that a half-hour a day of my time was worth whatever it meant to him. As long as I didn't look at him while he was eating.

I was leaving school Thursday afternoon when someone called my name. I turned around to see this girl coming toward me. She was smiling, and very pretty. I looked behind me, thinking I'd misheard her, but there was no one there.

"Hi, Tyler," she said.

"Uh, hi," I said.

"I'm Tara, Joey's sister. I just wanted you to know how sweet I think it is that you stood up for him. It's not easy for him, and my parents said to say thank you. Okay?"

"Oh, uh, yeah, sure. It's nothing," I replied. Her eyes, when I glanced at them, were such a deep green they made me dizzy.

"No, it's something," she said.

"Okay," I said.

"Well, I'll see you around?"

"Okay," I said. I walked away but only made it a few steps.

"Hey, Tyler," Tara said. I turned around, and she walked up to me. She smelled like flowers. I didn't say anything.

"I'm having a party at my place this weekend. Would you like to come?"

"Okay," I said. I felt like running away.

"Great!" she said. "Hey, what's your cell number?"

"Okay," I said. "No, I mean I don't have one."

"Oh, well, I'll see you around," she said.

"Okay," I said. I walked home wondering what I'd just done.

After supper I went to my room and lay on my bed wondering why I'd said yes to the party. It was obvious I didn't know how to talk to girls, unless "okay" was okay. And I couldn't smile even if I wanted to, with my teeth all messed up. I wanted to smash Dad's face in. Maybe I just wouldn't show up.

By the time Wayne called me for my workout, I was wired with rage. I did a total of ten rounds, four of them sparring. I poured all of my anger into the workout. Twice while Wayne held the pads for me I ripped one right off his hand. In sparring I kept him so busy defending against a blizzard of punches that he could hardly find time to counterpunch me. After the glove work was over, I punished my muscles with the weights, finishing up by pumping out reps on the bench press until I was in agony.

Wayne had started teaching me to play chess, so after a shower I challenged him to a game. It was all about strategy, and I liked the way it mimicked boxing. You had to attack, but you had to defend yourself too.

"You're ready, you know," Wayne said as I pondered a move.

"Yeah?" I asked absently, trying to keep focused on the maze of danger he'd spread across the board.

"To fight, I mean, for real," he said.

"Seriously?" I asked. I tried to sound casual, but my voice gave me away.

"Yes, but first I'd like to take you down to Shelburne for some real sparring. You can test yourself out on some active fighters. We'll do that twice a week, and I'll talk to some of the guys I know in the organizational end of things. So, probably within a month or so. Oh yeah, checkmate."

He'd left me an easy opening, and I'd fallen for it, the victim of my own aggression.

"If you think I'm ready, sure," I replied, my stomach fluttering with excitement. It felt a lot like fear.

The very next evening Wayne and I made the hour-long drive to the boxing club in Shelburne. We went down the rickety stairs to the basement and stepped into a huge room full of boxing equipment. Guys were hitting pads and bags, skipping rope, and shadowboxing everywhere I looked. There was also a seriously intense sparring session going on in the ring. I would have to earn any respect that I'd be given, but I was ready.

Wayne introduced me to a guy named Jed, who ran the club. He pointed to the locker room and told me to get changed. I felt like a real fighter, with my gym bag in my hand, and everyone sneaking peeks at me, trying to size me up.

I put on my protective cup and trunks, and wrapped my hands. Wayne fetched a pair of focus pads, and we warmed up for two rounds, just getting loose and ready for battle. Jed came over and handed me a pair of sparring gloves and nodded toward a guy across the room, telling me that we'd be doing two rounds, and to just take it easy.

Suddenly the ring was clear, and I stepped through the ropes. The other guy was about three inches shorter than me, but heavier, with a weightlifter's upper body. I'd watched him warm up, and saw that he threw hooks and straight rights and very few jabs.

The ten-second warning buzzer sounded, and Wayne said, "He's a slugger, so let him lead. Snap the jab, and give him lots of lateral movement. And keep your elbows in tight, he's a body banger. See you in three."

The bell rang and I shuffled straight toward him, then faded to my left, and he winged a right hook at my head. I slipped it and countered with a short hook of my own, scoring solidly. He recovered and squared up with me, then let loose with a flurry of arcing punches to my head and body. I blocked most of them, popping him with short and straight punches from both hands in retaliation. I could see that he was quickly losing his cool.

The harder he tried to take my head off, the easier it was to counter him. By the end of the round he had a small trickle of blood leaking from one nostril, and when the bell rang he tried to sucker me with a late punch. Back in the corner Wayne towelled the sweat off my face and gave me a drink of water.

"He's mad now, and a mad fighter's a beaten fighter. He's going to try to take you down. Have some fun, run some combinations, and keep your feet moving. By the way, that guy's had three fights. Won them all by knockout."

As Wayne had predicted, he tried even harder to hammer me down. He was loading up on his punches so badly that I could actually reach out and catch them on my open gloves as he let them fly. He was exhausted and hanging on by the time the bell rang.

Jed came over and clapped me on the

shoulder. "I guess I should've listened to Conway when he told me you were a natural. You're ready, that's for sure. We got a fight card coming up next week, but let's wait until the next one, two weeks before the holidays."

I was fairly floating from the adrenaline rush and from what Jed had said about me. The other fighters were looking at me in a whole different way now. I slipped on my gloves and prepared to hit the heavy bag. Two bags away was another guy, Aaron, I heard someone say. He was about my age and size, and was getting ready also. We both went all out for two rounds, and the gym echoed with the flat crack of leather on leather. When we finished I gave him a nod, and he smiled and winked. I hoped he wasn't going to be my first opponent.

I finished up with skipping and shadowboxing, then a brutal abdominal workout. Wayne and Jed warmed up and sparred three spirited rounds. Well, spirited for old guys. I changed back into street clothes and then went and shook hands with the guy I'd sparred earlier. I could tell he really didn't want to shake my hand, but he also didn't want to look like a sore loser.

"Training changes now, Tyler," Wayne said as we started for home. "You'll ease up on the weights, and we'll focus more on the pads and sparring. Just remember, it's all up here now," he said, tapping his head. "That's where your real strength resides."

My strength *and* my weakness. Just like it said in *The Art of War*.

# 20

## JAB BAG

We got back home at ten, and I went straight to my room. I tried reading but could only think of Tara. She had to know who I was, yet she still seemed interested. Maybe she liked the thought that I was dangerous. Like I was a bad guy. Then I realized how stupid that was. She liked me because I'd been kind to her brother.

I'd spent my whole life until now distinguishing myself as a tough guy. Now I had a new life with the Conways, and a smart, pretty girl was interested in me. And neither occurrence had anything to do with being tough.

Wayne and I started the new workout routine, where I was doing two rounds of shadowboxing, two rounds on the pads, and sparring four rounds every day. Then I'd do an intense abdominal workout and finish up with skipping. Plus, I ran every morning for at least a half-hour.

Everything was focused on pure boxing skills now. Wayne explained that anyone can punch hard enough to score a knockout, but you have to *land* those punches. And to do that takes skill. So I worked on speed and balance and throwing smooth combinations while on the move. And the jab. Always the jab.

Wayne had started fighting in different styles, sometimes in a new one for each round that we boxed. Some rounds he'd charge me, all elbows and shoulders. Sometimes he would make me chase him while popping fast jabs in my face. Sometimes he even turned southpaw, and I'd get hit with weird punches that I never saw coming. But always, the jab would be the punch that opened the way for me to solve the style he'd chosen.

Wayne had gotten a special bag, about the size of a soccer ball and filled with sand, made at the leather shop in town. He hung it from a rafter, level with my chin.

"It's a jab bag," he said. "I want you to work it every day, after you've finished ev-erything else. Do at least a hundred jabs, and practise snapping the punch, stepping right into it. Then practise the same thing fading away. I want that jab to make your opponents think you tossed a brick into their face."

I got my teeth replaced early Friday after-noon. Wayne said they were taken care of by the Family Services people, which was fine with me. The dentist explained that the new ones were bonded onto the stubs of the old ones and were just as strong as normal teeth. Wayne and I stopped at the sporting goods store on the way home for a new mouthpiece for me, since the old one wouldn't fit anymore. The mouthpiece was form-fitted by dropping it into boiling water, then placing it in your mouth and biting down on it. It molded so tightly to your teeth that you had to pry it out of your mouth when you were finished with it.

I spent the afternoon trying to relax. Girls were scarier than taking on two guys in a street fight. At supper Charlene asked me if I was all right, since I was just playing with my food. I said my stomach was upset, since it was. Wayne said we should skip the work-out anyway, on the dentist's advice. I wished I could get high.

I showered and got dressed for the party, and was ready by eight. I told Charlene and Wayne I was going out. They seemed curious but didn't ask any questions. I walked to the cor-ner of the street Tara lived on, then turned the other way. I went around the block, returned to the corner, then stood there, sweating.

All I had to do was walk up the street to her house and go in. Everything would be fine. I wouldn't have to talk much, I could just focus on responding to people, keeping it short. I started walking, breathing slow and steady. I was halfway up the block when I realized it was the first party I would be attending since I was seven.

I turned and went home.

# TOE TO TOE

On Monday it was back to training, and the weeks disappeared in a blur of flying fists and sweat. Running in the mornings, going to school, training, sleeping, then doing it all over again. I loved it. We went to Shelburne on Mondays and Thursdays to spar. I would do ten or twelve rounds against anyone from bantamweight to heavyweight. In the week leading up to my fight, the only person that I sparred with was Wayne, and that was only on Tuesday and Wednesday.

I called Tara to apologize about the party, my heart beating too fast and my voice shaky.

She asked me if I wanted to walk to school with her the next day. I did.

I met her at her house, and although I couldn't think of much to say, it wasn't a problem. She talked the whole way to school, although I didn't really hear much of what she said. I never knew someone could smell so good.

The two days before the fight were recovery days, so I took long walks in the mornings, shadowboxed, then walked again in the evening. Wayne walked with me in the mornings, and we talked about boxing, mostly the mental aspect of the sport. I didn't tell him that I was scared to death.

We had to be in Shelburne by ten o'clock Saturday morning. I barely slept the night before and was sorry I'd ever thought I could be a fighter. I couldn't lose. If I did, I would be ruined. I pictured myself getting whacked out really fast, and everyone laughing at what a fool I was.

I climbed out of bed feeling physically and

mentally weak, wondering if maybe I had the flu. I managed to eat breakfast, but Wayne could see how nervous I was.

"Let's take a walk," he said.

"Hold up, Tyler," he said after we'd gone a short distance. I stopped, imagining that for some reason, any reason, he was about to cancel the fight. Maybe he'd changed his mind and didn't think that I was prepared yet. I wouldn't argue with him.

"I know how you're feeling, and it's no different then what *every* fighter feels before their first fight," he said. "Heck, every fight, really. It gets a little easier to handle as time goes by, but it's still the same doubts and fears every time. Always remember that the guy across the ring from you is feeling the same way. The first and toughest foe you need to overcome is yourself. That's the real battle."

"You think I can do it?" I asked, hating the tremor in my voice.

"You're in better shape, and more talented, than any first-time fighter I've ever seen. You just have to believe in yourself, in who you are. In *what* you are. I'll see you back at the house."

I watched him go, then wandered along the trail, thinking of all the miles I'd run there, and for what? I knew I couldn't do it, and that I'd have no choice but to leave the Conways. I wouldn't live with their sympathy.

I returned to the house, and did a last-minute check to make sure that I had all of my gear. Charlene hugged me goodbye, since she wouldn't be going to the fight. I was glad about that.

"Just do your best, okay, Tyler?" she said. I lied and told her that I would.

We arrived at the club for the weigh-in, and I was sure that the other fighters weren't scared. Most of them were joking and horsing around. When I stepped onto the scale my knees were trembling, even though I wasn't worried about getting beaten anymore.

Wayne and I had an early lunch, since the fight card started at one o'clock. I was scheduled to go on second, so at twelve-thirty we warmed up on the pads. Wayne kept telling me to relax, and reminding me what great shape I was in. I wanted to hit him. The first fight went on, and I was next. I could hear the screams and yells from the crowd all the way back in the locker room, and I knew they were calling for blood. Anybody's blood.

"Time to glove up," Wayne said. And then I was walking toward the ring.

# SHADOWBOXING

The recreation centre was packed. I felt every eye on me as I ducked through the ropes into the ring. My legs were so weak I nearly fell down.

"My mouthpiece," I said to Wayne. "I forgot my mouthpiece." I couldn't fight without one.

"No problem, I brought a backup," he said, reaching into his shirt pocket. "The dentist did an imprint while you were there. He made you two. I picked them up yesterday."

The referee called us to the centre of the ring. I felt like I was moving under water.

Everything, the crowd, the noise, my opponent, faded into a blur as the referee gave us instructions.

Then I was back in the corner, weak and useless and scared stupid again. Just like Dad had always said. The bell rang and I waded forward, straight into the first punch my opponent threw. I heard a distant thudding sound, and the ring ropes seemed to reach out and pin me to them. Four more shots left my head whipping from side to side, and the referee jumped between us.

As he gave me an eight count, I gazed out at the people in the crowd, seeing a look of satisfaction on their faces. I was being hurt and humiliated again, and this time there was a crowd to enjoy it.

The ref signalled for us to continue, and I tried to move, but my legs refused. I got pinned and pummelled against the ropes again. I couldn't get my hands to work, and I couldn't even see the punches coming, as if I were in the dark. The referee separated us again, giving me another eight count while the crowd whooped and laughed. When he'd finished the count he asked me very quietly if I wanted to continue.

"One more eight count and it's over," he said. "I know you came here to fight, so come on, defend yourself."

I backed up against the ropes, tucking in behind my gloves and arms as my opponent continued to flail away at me. The referee yelled, "Break!" and I figured that was it, he was stopping the fight.

Instead, he pushed the other guy back and waved us together again. The first punch that came at me was a looping right, and it missed. On instinct I slipped it and countered with a tight hook to the body. He grunted and lifted one knee, then moved away. He recovered quickly and continued to pour on the punches, but I blocked most of them.

The bell rang, and I went back to my corner. Wayne smashed the stool down onto the floor and barked, "Sit!" He squatted down in front of me and pulled my mouthpiece out.

"Yes, I'm mad, but not at you," he said. "You *know* who's beating you, son. I know what he did to you, but you don't have to let him win, Tyler. You can go back out there and defeat him right now."

He gave me a drink of water, and I thought about what he'd said. I'd waited for years, ever since I was a little kid, for the chance to beat Dad. I *could* beat him, by winning this fight. I could prove that he'd been wrong about me all along.

"Okay," Wayne said. "Over in his corner, they're telling him to nail you with a big right hand. He's completely exhausted, look at him. As soon as he cocks his shoulder, throw the hook to the body. Don't think about it, just do it. Okay?"

I looked across the ring, seeing my opponent smiling at whatever was being said. He didn't look that tired to me.

He was rolling his shoulders and smirking as we approached the middle of the ring. Still, he was gasping for breath. He cocked his right hand, just as Wayne had predicted, and I closed my eyes and threw a hook to his body. The crowd exploded, and I looked down to see my opponent writhing on the floor. He was clutching his side and wheezing loudly.

The ref sent me to a neutral corner and picked up the count. At seven he stopped counting and waved that the fight was over.

The crowd went wild, and I went to my corner. Wayne jumped into the ring and hugged me, then stepped back and said, "You did it, Tyler. You beat him." I knew who he meant.

The ref came over and raised my hand as the ring announcer declared me the winner. I was handed a trophy and returned to the locker room with people clapping for me all the way back. They'd never know the real victory I'd won. Still, I knew it was a lucky punch.

I changed and returned to the floor of the arena, where we watched the rest of the fights. People kept coming up to me offering congratulations and telling me that they'd been cheering for me. I thanked each one of them, although I knew the truth. In that first round, these very same people had been yelling for my destruction. The best compliment came from an older guy with a flat nose and scarred eyebrows who told me I had heart.

Wayne was proud of me, or maybe it was more that he was proud *for* me. I could see it in his face. We climbed into the truck and started home. *Home*, I thought, holding my trophy in my lap.

"I know what you did out there today, Tyler," he said. "You overcame fear, and yourself, and that's the big victory. No matter what had happened, you would've still won. Because now you're not afraid to try, and that's what takes courage in life — the trying."

# BREAK

Charlene was waiting when we got home, all concerned because my face was swollen. I was proud of it. I ended up holding a towel full of ice cubes to my face, just to please her. It wasn't actually swollen, more like a little puffy.

After we'd eaten, Charlene decided she wanted to go to the mall and look for Christmas gifts. When we got there, we agreed to meet back at the main doors in one hour, and I wandered off on my own.

I was ten minutes early back to the doors. Wayne looked right at me, and then turned to say something to Charlene. After about three seconds he spun back to me, laughing out loud. He hadn't recognized me.

I'd gotten my hair cut for the first time since I was eight years old. I had trimmed it myself before, but I'd always kept the ponytail. This time I'd gotten it buzzed right down to the skull, though, because it was time to start over.

I had the ponytail in my jacket pocket. It was going on my wall, a reminder of how wrong Dad had been about me.

***

I slipped down to the mall and back in a taxi one evening while Wayne and Charlene were out, and bought their Christmas gifts. It was my first real Christmas. I didn't wake up sad, and no one got drunk and kicked the tree over.

I'd gotten Charlene a painting of a rose bush growing along a low stone wall. It was just like the one in her yard, except that she could look at this one all year long. I got Wayne an old-fashioned oil lamp, to sit on the mantel of the fireplace in his library.

I'd bought Tara a toque and scarf, the same green as her eyes, and Charlene wrapped them for me. I walked over to Tara's house one evening and left her gift on the porch. I didn't care if she got me anything. Her friendship was enough.

It was like magic in the Conway house, with all of the decorations twinkling in the glow of the multicoloured Christmas-tree lights. There were candle flames dancing atop the mantel, and wood crackling in the fireplace below. I wondered how Dad was doing.

\*\*\*

After the new year rolled in and everything had gotten back to normal, I had my second fight. I was nervous but not scared. Well, yeah, scared, but not like the first time. The guy I went up against was fast, but really tall and thin, and after the first round he returned to his corner bent over in pain. I'd listened to Wayne and waited until he'd thrown his jab, slipping under it to hammer his body. I was just standing up for the second round when the referee approached and informed us that the fight was over.

The guy that I'd had the heavy-bag show-down with at the gym in Shelburne, Aaron, fought right after me. I hurried out to see him, because I'd heard he was good. It was true; he looked like a pro and flattened his oppon-ent with one left hand halfway into the first round. I knew I would meet him somewhere along the line, and that it would take a lot of skill to beat him.

The next week I had my court date. Stand-ing in front of the judge, who held total control over my life, reminded me of life with Dad. He cleared his throat and peered at me over his glasses, and I was sure he was about to send me to jail.

"You're a lucky young man," he said. "You've got good people standing behind you, people who believe in you. You now have a chance to move forward. Don't waste it. I could sentence you to incarceration, but I won't. If I see you before me again, I will. Do you understand the break you're getting?"

"Yes, sir," I said.

Then he sentenced me to eighteen months' probation. I would have a curfew and report to a probation officer every week. All that really mattered now was proving that the Conways were right about me: I was worth saving.

\*\*\*

After a workout one night in late April, Wayne told me that he had my fifth fight lined up in three weeks. The surprise was that it would be at home, in Trenton, even though we didn't have a club of our own. I told Tara she couldn't come, and she laughed and said she loved it when I was stern. I couldn't help but wonder if Dad would hear and make the trip over from Rock Creek.

# GOING THE DISTANCE

Every morning now I went over to Tara's house, and we walked to school together. We went to a movie one Saturday night, and when I had walked her to her door she seemed nervous. We weren't an official couple, so I felt sorry for her. I knew she wanted to tell me that we couldn't hang out anymore. She was really out of my league. I was way wrong.

"I really like you, Tyler," she said. "You're different." Then she kissed me. I could still feel it when I got up the next morning. She was proof that I'd become normal. That my life had become normal. But still, I couldn't erase the ghost of Dad from my mind.

The three weeks flew by, and suddenly it was time to fight again. Before I knew it, the night of the fight had come. I was warming up in the locker room when an official came in to announce the matchups. There was too much noise, and we missed my opponent's name. Wayne asked for the name again, but the official was yelling out to someone across the room by then and didn't hear him. It didn't matter anyway. I was there to fight.

I went on third and walked to the ring, already sweating from my warm-up. Waiting in the ring was Aaron. My stomach lurched, but I swallowed hard and braced myself for a war.

I was introduced first, and it sounded like everyone in the crowd was yelling for me. Then Aaron was introduced, and the same thing happened. I scanned the crowd, looking for Dad, just hoping he might be there, but didn't see him. Tara and Joey were there, and she looked as frightened as if *she* were about to do battle.

Aaron and I met at ring centre, and I stared directly into his eyes as the referee gave us instructions. I was looking for that slightly skittish look that told if a fighter was worried. All I got was a smile, and I smiled back.

In the corner, Wayne told me to do what he *always* said to do: throw the jab, hit to the body, and move. Let the other guy come forward and then pick him apart with counter-punches. So far it had worked.

At the bell Aaron came straight toward me, looking like he was going to fire a big left hand, but I knew he was trying to trick me. He wasn't. It hit me flush in the face, and I countered with a right hook to the ribs. I faded away to his left, but he'd seen me fight and didn't make the mistake of reaching for me. Instead, he stepped to my right and fired a five-punch combination. Two of the punches landed, and then he was gone before I could recover.

I followed him, and he stayed just outside my reach as he whipped jabs at me. It was like his fist was steel and my face a magnet. Before the round was over my lips were numb. Just before the bell I trapped him against the ropes and we traded punches wildly as the crowd screamed.

"Get under the jab and pound that body. He has to protect it, so watch for a clean head shot. Keep him guessing," Wayne said as I tried to get my breath back. "You need this round."

I kept my hands up and started whipping jabs at Aaron's face to start the second round. He slipped a lot of them, and the ones that I landed didn't seem to faze him. He just kept countering me with left hands and stinging right hooks. I knew that I had to change tactics.

I bit down on my mouthpiece and charged, trapping him against the ropes. I fired punches non-stop, not even aiming them. He still countered, but I kept him pinned there, outscoring him until he casually spun clear near the end of the round. He hit me with a flurry of shots just as the bell rang. We returned to our corners as the crowd yelled for more. I flopped down onto the stool, aware that I'd made a mistake. I'd gotten too excited and had forgotten to breathe properly.

"You won that one, Tyler," Wayne said as he wiped my face. As soon as he moved the towel a fresh wave of sweat slid down my forehead, stinging my eyes.

"This is the round that counts. Just do your best. He's as tired as you are."

He wasn't. I knew that he'd been relaxing against the ropes, saving his energy while I threw everything I had. The minute-long rest between rounds wasn't long enough to recover, and when the ten-second call came my chest was still heaving. I had a fleeting thought of claiming an injury. That was the old me, the quitter, and I moved across the ring toward him on cement legs.

Aaron met me with a whipping jab, then got up on his toes and peppered me with dozens more as I tried to close the gap between us. I fired a wild left, hoping, and found myself sitting on the canvas. I hadn't seen the punch. I got up too fast and almost toppled over, and the referee looked me over carefully as he counted.

He waved us back in, and I landed a body shot that allowed me to clinch. Aaron stayed relaxed, letting the ref break us apart, then got back on his toes and rained punches on me again. I covered up, finally seeing an opening for a hook to the head, and let fly. He beat me to it with a hook to the body that felt like hot coals in my guts. I slowly sank to one knee, trying to get a breath into my lungs.

I looked at Wayne, who nodded at me. I looked at Tara, who was about to burst into tears. I managed not to puke as I rose at the count of seven. I lied to the ref when he asked me if I was okay.

"You sure, son?" he said, leaning in close so that only I could hear him over the screaming crowd. "I can stop it if you want."

"No!" I replied, slamming my gloves together. He waved us back in.

I kept looking for the big punch that would take Aaron out. If he knocked me down again the fight was over. When I knew that I couldn't stay on my feet much longer I threw a wild left hand that landed on his shoulder and knocked him into the ropes. He stepped to the left and nailed me on the chin with a hook. I staggered, and he smashed a straight right into my face. I wobbled sideways, letting go with a wide left, and caught him on the chin. He dropped but sprung back up.

I didn't hear the bell. The ring was filling with people and Wayne had his arm around my shoulders, leading me back to the corner.

"Did I do it?" I gasped.

"Yes, son, you did it," he said. He knew what I'd meant. I'd proven myself, and I'd proven Dad wrong.

I leaned on the ropes, heaving for breath and hoping that I wouldn't vomit. There seemed to be some sort of delay as the score-cards were added up. I hoped that they got the decision right. They did.

The referee called us to ring centre and raised Aaron's hand. I clapped along with the crowd, comfortable with having done my best. I'd proven more to myself than I had with any of my wins. I went to the locker room and changed, then went back out and sat with Joey and Tara. She hugged me and touched my face gently. Joey just wanted an ice-cream sandwich.

The next day my face was puffy and one eye was swelled half shut. I sat down with the Conways and explained that I no longer felt like I needed to prove myself. I was giving up boxing. Charlene was thrilled with my decision, but the big surprise was that Wayne felt the same way.

"You proved everything that you needed to in that first fight anyway, Tyler," he said. "You overcame fear, the thing that cripples more lives than anything. I'm really proud of you. We both are."

There was only one challenge left to overcome. One more thing to do so that I could walk away from my past.

# KNOCKOUT PUNCH

I had to go see Dad. I wanted to tell him that he'd lost, that I'd become everything that he'd said I wasn't.

Wayne agreed to drive me to Rock Creek, and we set out on a Saturday morning. We were both tense and quiet as the miles rolled by, until finally a road sign welcomed us to town. As soon as I saw the house it all came rushing back. I started to shake, and my heart was racing as I tried to breathe normally.

There was a truck parked by the house, slumped over on two flat tires, weeds growing up over the fenders. The house looked like it had been abandoned. There was cardboard taped over a broken window, and the roof was repaired with tarpaper patches.

Wayne parked on the street, and I got out of the truck and walked into the yard. Memories flooded my mind, and I could hear doors slamming and bottles smashing. I could almost smell the fear that always foreshadowed the violence. I went up the steps, opening the door without knocking, and stepped into the kitchen. There were empty liquor bottles everywhere, and the filth and stink of the place made me gag as I inched toward the living room.

He was sitting on the couch, thin and unshaven, in filthy and rumpled clothes. The whites of his eyes were yellow as he peered at me, and he'd wet his pants. He leaned forward to reach for a beer bottle on the coffee table but toppled to the floor.

"I made you tough, boy," he said as he unfastened his belt. He lay there, tugging at it, then gave up in a fit of coughing. I never felt so sorry for anyone in my life.

I walked over to him, bending down and standing him up. There was nothing to him. This was what I'd waited for, a chance to square things up. I sat him in the chair and stepped back. He closed his eyes and grimaced, like he was waiting for the blow he knew was coming.

"Can I do anything for you?" I asked.

"You can go to hell," he rasped.

As I went down the steps I noticed that the door to the shed was hanging open. The shed I had been warned never to go near. The hatchet from my nightmares still hung next to the door, the head rusted and the handle rotted. I walked over and peered inside. As my eyes slowly adjusted to gloom, I saw something hanging from a spike embedded in the wall. It was my bike.

I walked away.